Lacey Wells is determined to leave the peninsula someday.

"What makes you think I don't like the lighthouse?" Lacey asked, taking Micah's hand.

Jeremiah snorted. "It's plain as the nose on your face you hate that lighthouse."

Micah, confused, looked from Lacey to Jeremiah.

Lacey sighed. "I do not hate the lighthouse. It's just. . . It's only a lighthouse. Why does everyone get so excited about it?"

"Our family has tended the lighthouse for fifty-four years," Micah said, proudly relaying the facts. "It's an important job and we're honored to do it."

Lacey gave a half-smile at the perfect display of family pride. She had repeated those words herself hundreds of times when she was small but as she grew, her voice held less conviction. Now, at nineteen, she was nearly persuaded that keeping the lighthouse was no honor at all. Rather, it meant sacrifice and isolation.

She had grown up the same way that her father had before her, cut off from regular schooling, from friends and parties, even from church services. Their lighthouse sat solidly atop a cliff at the peak of the peninsula and to get to it by land took courage and determination. Perhaps that would change someday as the lumber industry and growing towns edged northward but for now crude roads threatened the axles of wagons and carriages and water breaks in the rugged ground could snap a horse's leg i

SUSANNAH HAYDEN is the pen name of a versatile and gifted author of fiction and biography for both adults and children. Susannah makes her home in Colorado Springs with her husband and children.

Books by Susannah Hayden

Tend
the Light

Susannah Hayden

Heartsong Presents

A note from the author:
I love to hear from my readers! You may correspond with me by writing: Susannah Hayden
                              Author Relations
                              PO Box 719
                              Uhrichsville, OH 44683

ISBN 1-57748-426-6

TEND THE LIGHT

Cover illustration by Victoria Lisi and Julius.

PRINTED IN THE U.S.A.

one

Lacey Wells pretended she did not hear them and, closing her eyes, she lifted her face to the spring sun and held still. She had not felt the sun on her skin for months. The northwestern Wisconsin winter had been long and harsh and twice her family had been snowed in and could not leave the lighthouse for days.

The bark of the tree that she was leaning against scratched through her calico dress but she paid it no attention. She felt only the crisp air cooling her cheeks and rustling the fine hair around her shoulders. Lacey sighed. Strands of her golden brown, wheat-colored hair had come loose and she moved her hand to brush her hair clear of her face.

In this place, this private clearing of the peninsula's forest, Lacey Wells could dream and imagine. Here no chores had to be done, no music lessons had to be endured, and every reminder of responsibility was out of sight. If she kept her blue-gray eyes low, she could not even see the lighthouse from this spot.

If only she could stay here all afternoon. But she heard them calling, even though she pretended not to. Still, she refused to answer. She knew that someday she would have to get off the peninsula.

Seven people in those small, awkward rooms of the lighthouse afforded little opportunity for thinking or dreaming. Because Lacey was the only daughter in the family, she had a tiny cubbyhole downstairs that she could call her own. Her parents were in the cramped room across the hallway from Lacey and her four brothers shared the large upstairs bedroom. Her mother never missed an opportunity to remind Lacey of her privileged privacy.

The shouts from her three little brothers were louder now

and they would find her in a few minutes. They were as eager as she was to be roaming the peninsula, escaping their mother's strict regimen of schooling. Three little boys could not be cooped up for weeks at a time without bursting the seams of rebellion and the coming of spring was the last push they needed to put them out on the land. Jeremiah and Joel were eleven-year-old twins always competing to lead the forays into the forest. Seven-year-old Micah trailed behind, knowing that he was allowed to come along only because their mother insisted that the twins include him; he mimicked everything they did.

Lacey could hear Jeremiah and Joel robustly shouting her name, demanding that she reveal herself. Micah's cry was thinner and less certain. In more sentimental moments, Lacey wanted to respond to Micah's voice, and she almost did today. But she stopped herself. If they wanted her, they would have to find her, even Micah.

"Why didn't you answer us?" Jeremiah demanded, bursting into the clearing.

Lacey reluctantly opened her eyes and confronted her brother. "I was busy."

"Doing what?" Joel wanted to know. "There's nothing to do here."

Lacy sighed. No answer she could give would satisfy Joel.

"Hi, Lacey," Micah said timidly.

"Hello, Micah," she answered, her voice softening slightly for the little blond boy. "What are you up to today?"

"Mama sent us for you," Micah explained.

Jeremiah twirled theatrically on one foot. "Mama says you've probably been daydreaming again." His arms swept over his head in a gesture of mock elegance.

"Stop it, Jeremiah!" Lacey said.

Jeremiah twirled again, and this time Joel joined him. "Mama says you're too fanciful for your own good."

"That's nonsense," she said.

"No, it's not. You can even ask Micah. Mama said so at

lunch today. She had to fix lunch all by herself, you know. You weren't there."

Lacey glared at her brother. "I imagined that one of you would offer to help."

"It's not my job to make lunch. That's your job. Mama says so."

"I wasn't hungry," Lacey said.

Joel snickered. "Mama said you would say that."

"Looks like she's got you figured out," Jeremiah added.

Lacey shook her head and rolled her eyes. "Why do you insist on bothering me so?"

"Mama sent us," Micah repeated.

"Time for you to come home," Joel said. "The supply boat's coming in. Papa saw it from the lighthouse."

"Of course, the lighthouse," Lacey muttered.

"Lacey?"

"Yes, Micah?"

"Why don't you like the lighthouse?"

"What makes you think I don't like the lighthouse?" Lacey asked, taking Micah's hand.

Jeremiah snorted. "It's plain as the nose on your face you hate that lighthouse."

Micah, confused, looked from Lacey to Jeremiah.

Lacey sighed. "I do not hate the lighthouse. It's just. . . It's only a lighthouse. Why does everyone get so excited about it?"

"Our family has tended the lighthouse for fifty-four years," Micah said, proudly relaying the facts. "It's an important job and we're honored to do it."

Lacey gave a half-smile at the perfect display of family pride. She had repeated those words herself hundreds of times when she was small but as she grew, her voice held less conviction. Now, at nineteen, she was nearly persuaded that keeping the lighthouse was no honor at all. Rather, it meant sacrifice and isolation.

She had grown up the same way that her father had before her, cut off from regular schooling, from friends and parties, even from church services. Their lighthouse sat solidly atop a cliff at the peak of the peninsula and to get to it by land took courage and determination. Perhaps that would change someday as the lumber industry and growing towns edged northward but for now crude roads threatened the axles of wagons and carriages and unseen breaks in the rugged ground could snap a horse's leg in an instant.

By water, the lighthouse was accessible for most of the year. A supply boat came every two months to bring the family flour, sugar, various dry goods, and, of course, oil for the lighthouse. During the winter the waters never quite froze but were, nevertheless, treacherous and rarely did anyone venture up to visit the Wells family during those months of short days and long nights. By November, supplies were laid in for the winter against the possibility that they would not be replenished until spring.

It was true that Lacey's father and her grandfather had been the lighthouse keepers for more than fifty years. Her sixteen-year-old brother, Joshua, would be next in line.

"Where's Joshua?" Lacey asked abruptly, remembering that the boys had come to tell her that the supply boat was arriving and that Joshua should be there to help unload.

"At the lumber camp."

"Again?" Lacey moaned. Joshua was spending every spare moment working at the lumber camp on the other side of the peninsula. He would quickly satisfy his mother's educational requirements and then be gone for days at a stretch. But whenever he was gone, Lacey seemed to inherit his share of the chores on top of her own.

"He'll be back tomorrow," Micah said, seeming to sense her irritation.

"Yes, but the boat is here today. We'd better go," she said.

Jeremiah and Joel immediately raced ahead of her, clearly glad to be rid of Micah. Lacey gave Micah's hand a squeeze, and he smiled up at her. "I like it when the boat comes," Micah said, "don't you, Lacey?"

She tried to respond as sincerely as he had asked the question. "Yes, it is a little exciting. We're never quite sure what Gordon will bring us."

"Mama says we really need flour and if he doesn't bring it, she's going to make him go back and get some!"

Lacey laughed. "I bet she will, too."

"Maybe if we hurry home, we can go up in the lighthouse and see the boat come around the bend."

Lacey nodded. "Sure, Micah. I'm sure Papa would let you go up today."

"I love the lighthouse," Micah said simply.

"That's nice." The last thing Lacey wanted to do was disillusion a seven-year-old child. "Maybe someday you'll be the keeper."

"Do you really think so? I hope so!"

When they were out of the clearing and on the path, Lacey raised her eyes to the lighthouse. The gleaming white tower with its bright red cap rose proudly above the craggy cliff just like it had for eight decades, since just before the dawn of the nineteenth century. The original circular wick that burned whale oil had been updated to four wicks burning vegetable oil and then kerosene. Daniel Wells had taken great pride in installing prisms that magnified the light as far as twenty miles. A railing, also painted red, circled the tower. Lacey's father had built a bench so he could sit and look over the railing, sometimes scanning for ships, sometimes. . . She was not sure what he did some of the time.

Lake Superior bent just at that point, and under the water the mountain of rock was less visible. Without the lighthouse, especially at night, it was next to impossible for a craft of any size to estimate distances and navigate around the curve. Aged and rotted wooden memorials dotted the far shore to mark the failures of the past.

Daniel Wells was as serious about maintaining the outside of the lighthouse as he was tending the light at the top and never did he postpone the upkeep or allow any blemish to obscure the visibility of the lighthouse. Tending the light was not simply the way he earned his living; it was a calling, which he answered enthusiastically.

Daniel Wells had grown up on the peninsula, learning from his own father how to keep the light burning and how to sound the foghorn in the darkness. His two sisters and one brother had left long ago, but he had stayed, never grumbling about the isolation or the difficulty of life on the peninsula. He had met his wife, Mary, on a blind date arranged by one of his sisters, and she had accepted the lot of a lighthouse keeper's wife. She raised her children in the house attached to the tower, insisting that they learn to read and appreciate literature and to play several musical instruments.

Several times Lacey had visited her grandmother's home in Milwaukee, where her mother had grown up. On her first visit she felt as though she were on a different planet with the spacious rooms, the wide streets, and the shops at the center of town. She could still hear her mother chastising, "Lacey, don't stare!"

Since her eighth birthday Lacey had known that someday after she finished high school she would go to a place like Milwaukee to stay. Now, three years after having finished high school, Lacey was even more determined to leave but, somehow, she had not made any serious plans to go. Her mother refused to let her go without some proper purpose for leaving; she also insisted that Lacey was still needed at home and certainly did not need to be wandering around the state unattended.

Micah was tugging her hand. "Let's hurry, Lacey. The twins will get there first and then Papa will say it's too crowded for me at the top."

Lacey stepped up her pace, playfully pulling Micah along.

two

"I see the boys found you," Mary Wells said to her daughter as Lacey and Micah reached the edge of the yard behind the house. "I could have used your help with lunch."

Lacey touched Micah's shoulder. "I'll see you down there," she said, sending him off scampering gladly toward the boat. Lacey made no response to her mother who was tossing another handful of feed to the chickens. Lacey wondered why Jeremiah had not done so earlier.

"Did Joel do the milking?" Lacey asked, glancing around for the cow.

"I had to remind him three times," her mother said. "There's butter to be churned this afternoon."

"I'll do it as soon as we finish unloading the boat," Lacey offered.

"Your father will be down in a few minutes with the cart," her mother said. "Go ahead and start unloading without him."

"If you give me the list," Lacey said, "I'll see if everything is there."

Her mother reached into the pocket of her apron and fished out a crumpled scrap of paper. "Make sure he leaves flour. We don't have enough to last until the next trip. And don't let the boys play with the ropes."

Without comment, Lacey turned away. Her mother gave the same warnings every time the supply boat came. Lacey scanned the list and she saw the usual items, dominated by the need for oil to keep the lamp burning at the top of the lighthouse.

❧

The rugged cliff rose up steeply from the supply boat. The

11

nearest place to actually dock a boat and and unload it was three miles away, around the bend. For years Daniel Wells had talked about carving out a road that would let them unload supplies on more level ground and carry them over the land. But the road was never made, so he and his sons used a network of pulleys and ropes to haul supplies up the cliff from the boat. Once, the twins had gotten their fingers caught in the ropes. Micah was forbidden to touch them, but he could not keep himself away from the unloading process.

Lacey did not share her brothers' passion for the supply boat, and she thought she was much too old to be forced to take part in the ritual unloading. But long ago she had accepted the task for it was not a point worth arguing with her mother. Mary Wells had a system for everything and her systems had worked well over the years to keep the family going in such an isolated place. But Lacey was ready to break out of the system.

The lighthouse, with their family home attached, sat right up at the edge of the cliff, so it took only a few steps for Lacey to reach the spot where the supplies would appear. A three-foot-high fence, painted luminescent white, marked the edge of the yard and the beginning of danger. Mary Wells had insisted that her husband build the fence before Lacey learned to walk; it had been freshly painted every summer since.

Joel and Jeremiah were already leaning on the pulley crank at the gate, moving a load. Micah chinned himself on the fence to survey the activity below. Lacey paused to stand behind him for a moment and she saw that the deck of the small boat was laden with barrels and crates. Lacey hoped for some new calicos.

"There she is, the love of my life," boomed a voice from the craft below.

Lacey rolled her eyes for Gordon Wright was the last person she wanted to see right then. Looking down over the edge of the cliff, she forced herself to say, "Hello, Gordon."

He grinned up at her from the ship's deck forty feet below, his sweaty face glinting in the sun and his mouth cockeyed.

"What do you say I take you for a nice boat ride today? The water's calm as can be." He had asked her the same question on every visit for the last three years, whether the water was calm or not.

"Thank you, Gordon, but not today. Have you got flour this time?" she asked.

Gordon snorted. "Flour. All your mama thinks about is flour. Does she think she's the only one in the world who needs it?"

"She has a family to feed," Lacey said. "We're not farmers; we can't grind our own."

"You never tried." He spat tobacco over the side of the boat. "Put in some wheat with those vegetables you always plant."

"Have you got the flour or not?"

"Why don't you come down and see for yourself?" His grin was turning into a leer.

"Gordon, please." She glanced at Micah's hopeful, innocent face. The boy was mesmerized with the pulleys and seemed not to notice the conversation. She moved away from the edge to where the twins were working the pulley.

"I'll come up and get you," Gordon persisted. "You can hang onto me all the way down. That rope ladder is sturdy enough for the two of us."

Lacey was glad he was out of her sight, even if just for a moment. "Just send up the flour or I'll go get my mother." Lacey yanked on a pulley, jerking Gordon's arm at the other end.

"Woman, what are you doing?" Gordon burst out. He scowled up at her. "Don't know why I waste my time chasing after you when any woman in town would be glad to be my bride. A man like me makes a good living around here."

"Don't be too sure about that," Lacey snapped.

The twins giggled at the exchange but Lacey paid no attention for it was all part of the ritual that they loved and she abhorred. Even when she was sixteen she had not been fooled by Gordon's attentions, though she had been the tiniest bit flattered. Now she was strictly annoyed. She glanced back over her shoulder, hoping her father would appear with the cart soon.

Lacey leaned into the pulley alongside Joel and Jeremiah, and a barrel of kerosene slowly crept up the side of the cliff. Cautiously, she looked over the edge to make sure Gordon was cooperating by tying on the next item. Fortunately, his back was to her as he sorted the crates.

As she watched his movements, another figure emerged from the hold of the ship. Usually, Gordon came alone for his was a small boat and he always made a point of letting people know he did not carry passengers. Had he hired some help? Lacey could not hear what the man said to Gordon, but she kept her eyes fastened on him. He was tall with broad shoulders and brown, thick curly hair, exuding a gentle quality that Gordon's friends did not usually have. He moved smoothly across the deck of the ship and laid a fifty-pound sack of flour at Gordon's feet. Somehow he did not strike Lacey as the type of man Gordon would bring along to help with the heavy load.

Lacey was determined to meet him. For a moment, she even thought of descending the rope ladder to the rickety dock, something she had not done since she was a little girl. Instead, she called down, "Hello!"

The man looked up. "Hello!" His dark eyes met her gaze.

"Are you a friend of Gordon's?" she asked.

The man smiled. "A passenger. How about you?"

She looked up, questioning.

"Are you a friend of Gordon's?" the man asked.

"We've known each other a long time," Lacey said awkwardly, perhaps not loud enough for him to hear.

The man turned back to his work, methodically moving supplies closer to the pulley so Gordon could unload them. Lacey and the boys continued winding. But it was hard to wind the pulley and look over the edge at the boat at the same time so Lacey had to surrender her curiosity to the immediate task.

"Look, he's coming up!" Micah squealed from his outpost.

Lacey's head shot up and she looked at the ladder. If Gordon came up, it would take all afternoon to get rid of him. She would rather risk her mother's wrath and abandon her task than have to stand face-to-face with Gordon Wright and endure his pawing and leering. But it was not Gordon. It was his passenger who had placed his foot securely in the bottom rung of the rope ladder and who, with a small pack tied to his back, gripped the ropes and skillfully maneuvered himself up the ladder.

"Push harder, Lacey," demanded Joel, pulling her back to the task at hand.

She cranked the pulley frantically, wanting to be free to greet the visitor. Out of the side of her eye, she caught his movements as he pulled himself up over the top, brushed himself off, and extended to his full height.

"Hello. I'm Travis Gates," he said.

"Lacey Wells," she responded, immediately wishing she had said something more creative.

"I've heard all about you. Gordon is quite smitten."

Lacey blushed, sweat trickling down one temple.

"Harder!" Joel insisted. "He's putting on another barrel of kerosene."

"Maybe I can help," Travis said as he moved in between Lacey and Joel.

Lacey hastily introduced her brothers. Travis's hand gripped the crank handle along with hers and together they turned it. Immediately the task eased, and in a few moments, the barrel tumbled over the top and the twins steadied it.

Lacey tried to steady herself. She did not know what to say to Travis Gates, but she wanted to say something. "Did you see any more flour on the boat?"

"Several sacks," he said.

Then Lacey glanced down to see Gordon loading another fifty-pound sack on the pulley. "Thank you for helping," she said.

"It's my pleasure."

"What have we here?" a voice asked.

Lacey spun on one heel to see her father behind her. "Papa, I didn't hear you." She faltered only a moment before regaining her poise. "This is Mr. Travis Gates. He's a passenger on Mr. Wright's boat."

Travis extended his hand to Daniel Wells. "Actually, I've reached my destination," he said.

"Well, then, welcome to the peninsula," Lacey said graciously, all the while wondering why anyone would choose to come to a place that felt like the end of the earth.

"What is your business here?" her father asked.

"I've come to work in the lumber camp for a few months." Travis offered no further explanation. "I'm told that I can find the road to the camp not far from the lighthouse."

"That's true," said Daniel Wells, "but the hike is several miles and the road is more like a trail. Why don't you come up to the house for some refreshment before starting out?"

"I would not want to inconvenience you," Travis said.

"It's not an inconvenience. We don't often have guests on this side of the peninsula. My wife will enjoy talking with someone from the city." He turned to his sons. "Joel, Jeremiah, Micah, run up and tell your mother we have a guest."

The twins groaned but Micah jumped to his feet. "I will!" he said and then he was off.

Travis glanced at the wooden cart that Daniel Wells had dragged to the cliff. "Can I help you load your goods?"

"We'll get it later," he said, looking at the barrels and crates his sons had dutifully lined up. "Looks like everything is there."

Lacey fumbled for the list wadded up in her hand. "Yes, it's all there. Enough oil for at least two months."

Her father leaned over and waved at Gordon. "Do you want to come up for some refreshment?"

Lacey's heart nearly stopped. Did her father always have

to be so hospitable? He knew how she felt about Gordon Wright.

"Daniel Wells, you don't know what real refreshment is," Gordon called up, laughing. "I'll just go back to where I can get a real drink. Tell your friend, Saget, that next time I'll have supplies for the lumber camp and I'll expect to be paid." Then he pushed his boat away from the edge and jumped on it.

Travis hoisted a sack of flour. "Perhaps I'll work my way into your wife's good graces if I deliver some flour."

Daniel Wells laughed. "Her reputation has preceded her, I see. But the need is genuine. With five children in the house, we go through it pretty fast."

"Five? I counted only four, including Lacey, that is."

Lacey was at the same time grateful and embarrassed by Travis's acknowledgement that she was not a child.

"My son, Joshua, is the fifth," Daniel Wells explained. "I imagine you'll meet him when you get over to the camp. He spends as much time there as he does at home." He raised his eyes to the side door of the little house. Mary Wells had opened it and stepped outside and Micah was at her side. "I see Mary is ready for us."

Lacey fell into step between Travis and her father.

three

Mary Wells, holding a pitcher, stood poised over Travis Gates.

"Thank you, yes." He held up his glass for a refill.

"So you've come to the peninsula for only a few months?" Daniel Wells resumed their conversation. Lacey waited eagerly for the answer.

"My schedule is rather indefinite," Travis replied, "but I expect I will be here less than a year, perhaps only until winter sets in again."

"Are you a lumberjack?" The question came from Micah, perched on his father's knee.

"Not exactly," Travis replied, tilting his head. "But I want to learn about it."

"My brother is a lumberjack," Micah boasted.

"Then maybe he can teach me," Travis said.

Lacey was bursting with questions. Most of the men who came to work at the lumber camp stayed there for years; she had not known anyone who came for only a few months. Also, Travis did not look like a lumberjack. Joshua did not look like a lumberjack, either, but he was still a boy. Travis was a man, in his midtwenties, Lacey estimated, with smooth hands and trimmed nails. Wherever he had come from, he had not made his living felling trees and hauling lumber.

"How do you know Gordon Wright?" Daniel Wells asked. "He's never been one to carry passengers."

Travis chuckled. "Well, it was a bit of a challenge to get him to take me, but he was paid well for it. He's an acquaintance of someone my father does business with."

"What kind of business is your father in?" Daniel Wells asked.

"Industry," Travis answered.

What kind of industry, Lacey wanted to know but she did not ask. Travis seemed relaxed in her family's home, yet at the same time he gave guarded answers that did not fully satisfy her curiosity.

Mary Wells took her seat. "Are you sure you can find the camp on your own? The light may fade before you get there."

Daniel Wells pushed back his chair and nudged Micah to his feet. "Mary is right. You should be on your way before it is too late to go today."

"Perhaps you could just point me toward the road," Travis said.

"I'll walk with you," Lacey said impulsively. She had not spoken much during the previous conversation and her mother now looked at her with raised eyebrows. Lacey continued, "Showing you will be easier than telling you how to find it."

"Yes, that's sensible," her father said.

Lacey glanced at her mother, who set her jaw but did not speak.

"Can I come, too?" Micah's hopeful blue eyes looked up at his father and Lacey's heart sank for she knew that expression was hard to resist.

Daniel Wells stroked the boy's head. "How about if you stay here and help me and the twins with the supplies?"

"Okay." Micah was easily diverted from one pleasure to another.

"I would be happy to help, too," Travis said.

Daniel Wells shook his head. "You'd better get going. I don't want you lost in the woods after dark."

"Well, all right, then." Travis stood up and smiled at Lacey. "Is my guide ready?"

Lacey felt the color rise in her cheeks, but she held her composure. Once outside, she gestured across the yard toward the edge of the forest. "This is the quickest way," she advised and then did not know what to say after that.

Travis came to the rescue. "Micah seems like a delightful child," he said as they fell into step together.

Lacey smiled, grateful to talk about something familiar. "He is. He's not like Joshua or the twins."

"They are not so delightful?" Travis teased.

"They're, you know, boys!" Lacey said emphatically. "Actually, Joshua is nearly grown and has turned into a like-able person, despite my doubts of a few years ago. I think you'll enjoy him. The twins, though, they're in their own world most of the time. Since they have each other, they don't seem to need anyone else."

"Least of all, Micah," Travis offered.

"Exactly. Mama tries to make them include Micah, but they avoid it whenever they can."

"I've never seen twins look so much alike!"

"If you spend anytime with them, you'll be able to tell them apart," Lacey said.

"I hope to have the opportunity."

Involuntarily, Lacey glanced sideways at Travis. Was he simply being polite?

Leaving the yard, their path began to wind around the trees and Travis said, "I can see how easy it would be to get lost."

"You'll get used to it," Lacey assured him. "The trail is used just enough to keep it beaten down. Joshua goes back and forth a couple of times a week." She looked at his profile. "Do you know anything about tracking?"

"Tracking?" He looked dubious.

Lacey laughed. "You really are a city boy, aren't you?"

"Guilty as charged," Travis said, also laughing. He gestured to his wide surroundings. "But this is beautiful. I'm going to love it here, I'm sure. It must have been wonderful growing up here."

"Funny, I was just about to say that about growing up in the city."

Travis shook his head. "Where I come from is not much of a city, really, just a town. People work too hard and drink too much. They forget to look at what's around them."

Lacey surveyed the familiar territory that had become her

prison without walls. "I guess it's all a matter of your perspective," she said quietly.

Travis glanced at her sideways. "Don't you like living here?"

"It's beautiful, no question about that. But it's. . ."

"Lonely?" Travis asked quietly.

She nodded.

"Have you no friends up here?"

"One," Lacey answered. "Abby Saget. Her father has been cutting wood for years. She grew up as the only child at the lumber camp. But the boys have never had any friends."

"At least they have each other, especially the twins."

"They don't see it that way. Having brothers is not the same as having friends."

"It is far away from a lot of things that I take for granted," Travis admitted. "School, church, friends. It must be hard for you sometimes."

Lacey wanted to shout that it was hard all the time, that she wanted nothing more than to leave the peninsula, that he was lucky he was only here for a few months. Instead, she simply said, "Yes, it can be hard."

"Have you lived here all your life?" Travis asked.

Lacey launched into her family's history of fifty-four years of tending the lighthouse, schooling at home, living miles away from playmates and hundreds of miles from relatives.

"Will Joshua take over the lighthouse, then?" Travis asked at the end of her explanation.

"That's what my father hopes."

"But what about the lumber camp?"

"I think Joshua is just trying to save up some money, something that he can call his own. My mother hates it that he goes to that camp. She would never stand for having him there all the time."

"Why does she hate it?"

Lacey shrugged. "She thinks it's an uncivilized way of life and not a suitable environment for her children."

"But Joshua is not a child."

"To Mama he always will be."

"I suppose mothers are that way. But perhaps it will not always be so uncivilized."

Lacey wondered what he meant. She had not seen much progress toward civility in her lifetime, certainly not any standard that would please her mother. The men slept in crude cabins without feminine influence, chewing and spitting what they pleased, and consuming a dubious diet. Moonshine flowed freely. Lacey wondered how someone like Travis Gates would fit in.

"Does your mother read the Bible a lot?" Travis asked.

Lacey was startled by the shift in conversation and furrowed her brow.

Travis explained. "Your brothers' names, three prophets and a courageous leader."

"Let's just say she made sure we learned our Bible stories, even without a church to go to."

"And your name? It's unique."

"Letitia, my grandmother's name." The truth was out before Lacey could stop herself. "But Joshua couldn't say it when he was little. The nickname stuck, especially after the twins were born."

"I like it."

Lacey laughed.

"What's so funny?" Travis asked.

"Some people have known me nearly all my life and they don't know my real name is Letitia. Even I hardly ever think about that. Yet I'm giving away my secrets to someone I hardly know."

"I assure you, your secret is safe with me."

Smiling, Lacey let the comment roll off and the conversation moved on to the habits of the squirrels darting across their path. Inwardly, though, Lacey replayed her interchange with this strange man. Why was she talking so freely to Travis Gates? After the conversation with her father back at the house and the discussion on the path, Travis knew a fair amount about the Wells family in general, and Lacey in particular. But, beyond his name, she knew practically nothing about him, not even the name of the town he had grown up in or the real reason why he had come to the peninsula. Was he hiding something or simply being casual? Intuitively, she did not believe that he had come to earn his fortune by cutting lumber.

"Gordon Wright is right, you know." Travis interrupted her reflective mood. "You have spunk."

Lacey slowed her steps and looked at Travis. "Gordon said that?"

"The exact quote is, 'That girl has more spunk than ten city girls rolled into one.' "

"I'm sure he was exaggerating. He drinks too much, you know."

"That much was easy to see. And when he drinks, he talks . . .about you."

"Why would Gordon do that?"

"He's stuck on you."

"Nonsense!"

"No, it's not nonsense."

"But he's a blathering, blubbering boob who has no idea what to say to a woman. Most of what he does say is offensive. I've never given him the least bit of encouragement."

"Doesn't matter."

"Oh, let's talk about something else," Lacey said, exasperated. Any other topic would be more interesting than an analysis of Gordon Wright's emotional state. "You know all about my family. Now, tell me about yours."

"Not much to tell. I'm an only child and my mother died when I was twelve. My father spent most of his time working while I was growing up."

Apparently, Travis intended to say no more. With a summary like that, Lacey was sure there was more to the story, much more. But she could not be pushy with a stranger.

"I'm sorry about your mother," she said softly.

Travis shrugged. "It was a long time ago."

They had come to her clearing and she stopped to lean against her favorite tree. "You can pick up the path right over there," she said, pointing to the other side. "After a mile or so, it curves a little to the north. Otherwise, it's pretty direct."

"I appreciate your bringing me this far," Travis said.

"I'm surprised someone didn't meet you," Lacey said.

Travis smiled slyly. "They didn't know I was coming today. And I'm told most of the men come over the land route from the southern part of the state."

"Yes, that's true," Lacey conceded, at the same time wondering why Travis had chosen the water route. "Well, I'm sure they'll be glad to have another pair of hands."

"I'll look for Joshua."

"Please do. My mother would like that. And I'm sure you'll meet Abby."

"Perhaps I'll see you again, Lacey Wells." His dark eyes held her for just a moment.

Lacey blushed. "Perhaps so." She looked away awkwardly.

With a final wave, Travis turned and headed for the path. Lacey watched him recede into the woods and, in only a couple of minutes, he was beyond her sight. Yet his presence lingered in the clearing and Lacey took a deep breath of his scent, manly, but not sweaty. She wondered what he would smell like after a stint in the camp.

She was tempted to settle in the grass for another private session in her clearing but it was not worth annoying Mama two times in one day. Mama would have calculated how long it would take for Lacey to walk Travis to the clearing and when she should be back. Besides, she had promised to churn the butter. Soon it would be time to get supper going, and if she was not there to help, Mama would send the boys after her again. Reluctantly, Lacey turned her feet back toward the lighthouse.

Travis's comments about Gordon hung in her mind. If she had so much spunk, more than ten city girls, why did she feel so trapped? A woman with spunk would have found a way off the peninsula by now, instead of going home for supper to avoid a scolding. But Lacey did not see that she had any options. Mama was not going to let her go without a good reason to leave, and so far Lacey had not been able to offer any that qualified. Even if her mother changed her mind tomorrow, what would Lacey do? Where would she go?

She kicked the dirt, wishing she at least had an answer that would satisfy herself.

four

The lilac would peel off the wall with the slightest touch, Lacey knew. No doubt her grandmother, for whom she was named, had lovingly papered this tiny room, hardly more than an alcove, with enthusiasm and expectation that it would bring pleasure to the occupants. And perhaps it had, at one point. Surely the wallpaper had been clean and vibrant in those days, the flowers brightening the walls as the breeze stirred the curtains. Lacey knew that her aunts, her father's sisters, had shared this small space while they grew up.

Now, however, the wallpaper was yellowed and cracked and the lilacs on one wall were so faded from the sunlight that they were barely visible. Lacey lay on her bed, with her arms thrown up over her head, and picked at the seam in the corner. She scraped at the paper's edge with her thumbnail as miniscule flakes scattered on her pillow. Years ago, she had gotten excited about redecorating her room and she had it all planned out. When they went to visit her mother's family in Milwaukee, they would buy new wallpaper, paint, and fabric. The room was tiny and it would not take much. She would do the work herself, from stripping the old wallpaper to pasting the new and carefully stroking paint onto the trim around the window and door. She had drawn a picture for her mother to show the color scheme she wanted.

Even now Lacey could see her mother's raised eyebrows for she thought the room was serviceable the way it was. Lacey needed to concentrate on her schoolwork and chores, not on changing something that did not need to be changed. But Mary Wells had finally relented and allowed Lacey to freshen the trim. The new paint, however, simply made the wallpaper look more dull and Lacey was sorry she had done it.

That was when she first became convinced that she needed to leave the peninsula, years before it would become possible. Daniel and Mary Wells had made a life for themselves here and they would never leave. But when Lacey pictured her future, she was always somewhere else in a place with people, activity, and maybe even a family of her own. When she was fourteen, she had determined that she would suffocate if she stayed here. But, at nineteen, she was still here.

Lacey swung her feet over the side of the bed, sat up, and sighed. The house was quiet. Her mother had sent the boys to their room hours ago and Micah had lain in bed singing until the twins made him stop with threats of physical harm. It was a nightly ritual, an argument that Lacey had grown weary of overhearing. After having sat in the living room with the mending pile for an hour or so, Mary had gone to bed herself.

The house was still but Lacey's mind was far from quiet as the events of the day tumbled through her mind, from her quiet hours in the clearing to the mysterious Travis Gates. At the supper table, everyone had had a comment to make about the newcomer. Jeremiah was impressed by his physical strength. Joel was suspicious that he was too good to be true and that distressed Micah. Daniel was impressed with his pleasant demeanor. Their mother took a let's-wait-and-see attitude. Lacey had not known what to think and she shared with her family very little of her conversation with Travis, thinking that probably she would not see him again, anyway. To Travis, she had simply been a young girl who could point him in the direction he needed to go, and he had been polite enough to make pleasant conversation along the way. Lacey had not even undressed for bed yet, somehow knowing that she would need to get up and go out. Now, she slipped her feet into her shoes and pulled a shawl around her shoulders for although the spring days were warm, the nights could be brisk.

In the kitchen, a lamp glowed softly on the table and that meant that her father had not yet gone to bed, either. No doubt he was up in the lighthouse now. In this way, Lacey and her father were more alike than anyone else in the family. Neither of them was able to leave the cares of the day and go to bed and fall instantly into a sound sleep. Lacey had been Micah's age when she began creeping out of her room after her mother was asleep to go see her father. Over the years, he had come to expect Lacey's visits, and Lacey took refuge in knowing that she could make them.

Lacey stepped outside the back door and looked up. The light in the tower burned fiercely bright against the black sky. Truly it was a beacon in the darkness to anyone on the water at night. In its yellow hue, Lacey could see her father leaning over the red railing encircling the peak of the tower. Had the night been much colder, he would have been inside the light room, but in fair weather he could not resist the railing. Daniel Wells was exactly where Lacey had expected to see him. From this distance, he looked oddly small; perhaps it was the overpowering presence of the light distorting his proportions.

Moving swiftly with the confidence of a long habit, she moved along the side of the stone house and let herself in through the small wooden doorway at the base of the lighthouse. Though the stairwell was pitch dark, she did not bother to light a candle for she knew the path well with each of its turns and upward curves. As she wound her way up, she let one hand drag along the cold stones.

When she emerged at the top, her father turned toward her. "Thought you might have been up here an hour ago."

Lacey smiled gently. "I should have come sooner. I knew I would not sleep tonight."

He turned his gaze back toward the water; a sliver of moonlight reflected on the water below. Intermittent clouds hid most of the stars, but the tower's light would have obscured them anyway. Lacey moved in next to her father and laid her head on his shoulder.

"How can you think this is not beautiful?" he asked softly.

"It is beautiful," she replied simply.

"But not beautiful enough? Not enough to hold you?"

Lacey sighed. "I do love the view from up here. But, no, it's not the same for me as it was for you. . .or for Grandfather."

"Ah, I had hoped it was in the blood of all my children. Nothing would give me greater pleasure than to have another generation of the Wells family tend this light."

Lacey did not respond. As much as she longed to leave the peninsula, she hated to disappoint her father. But she was not his only child. Perhaps Micah's passion for the family heritage would survive his adolescence.

"Your mother tells me you will not be with us much longer," he said quietly.

Lacey snapped her head around to look at him in disbelief. "She said that?"

He nodded.

"But. . .I don't understand. When I wanted to go last year, she wouldn't let me."

"She didn't think you were ready."

"Because I had no husband?"

"Because you had no purpose, except to leave. She just didn't think you were ready."

"But how will I know what purpose might be out there until I go?" Lacey protested. "Why can't she understand that?"

"Your mother has developed some harsh ways over the years. It's my fault, I guess, for bringing her here and expecting she would love it as much as I do."

"Doesn't she?"

He shook his head. "No, but she has made a life for us all anyway, and I'm grateful for that. But she knows that she cannot hold any of you here. The time will come."

"Does she really talk to you about these things?"

He looked at his daughter and chuckled. "Do you really think we're so old and feeble that we cannot sustain a conversation about our children?"

Now Lacey laughed. "I'm sorry. I sound ridiculous. But Mama. . .she is so strict and hard to please."

"She is that way because she wants you to be prepared when the time comes."

Lacey was silent. She had never thought of her mother's viewpoint, instead focusing only on her own inner struggle for a place to belong. "Why does she think I'm ready to leave now?"

"Not now," he corrected, "but soon. I'm afraid that's a question you'll have to ask her."

"Did you ever think about leaving, Papa?"

He shook his head slowly. "Briefly, when I was twelve and your grandmother, Letitia, tore up my favorite shirt for a rag. But I could never leave, not really. I was fortunate enough to have found someone willing to come here, instead of making me choose between the peninsula and a home and family."

They fell into silence, Lacey pondering her father's last comment. For her, such a choice would be simple: leave the peninsula. But she knew that her father's heart would have been wrenched out of him if he had had to face such a choice. His calling, his dedication were a mystery she admired but never hoped to understand.

"Gordon Wright would take you away, you know," he said.

"Papa! That's nonsense."

"I don't think so."

"But I could never. . .ugh! I'd be just as happy if he never spoke to me again."

"I'm not saying he's perfect, but he does have some redeeming qualities."

"Such as?"

"He works hard and he makes a good living. He also adores children. He's a little rough around the edges, but I think that's because he genuinely cares about you and doesn't know how to express himself. If you were to—"

Lacey cut him off. "Papa, you're not suggesting—"

"I'm not suggesting anything, Lacey. How you respond to

Gordon Wright is your decision. But whatever you do, be sure to look beneath the surface."

Lacey got his point. More than once she had been accused of impetuousness and hasty decisions. No doubt this was one of the reasons her mother was so firm with her, even though she was nineteen years old.

"Papa, don't you ever wonder what else is out there?" she asked.

"Sure, sometimes," he answered. "But there is so much here and I feel no urgency about what else there is out there."

Lacey stared into the night. Below them the water slapped the rocks and reminded them of hazards that had demanded a lighthouse in that place. Together they soaked up the nighttime beauty and their closeness. Unlike her father, though, Lacey felt the urgency.

five

Having gratefully escaped from her mother's watchful eye, Lacey had spent most of the day with Abby Saget, her best friend, really her only friend. But, right now, if Lacey could have picked up a tree and thrown it across the forest, she would have. Had Abby lost her mind?

Abby's father, Tom Saget, managed the lumber camp and Abby had grown up on the other side of the peninsula and much closer to the camp than the Wells family. Tom Saget had been consistently discouraged from bringing his wife and daughter to the camp and for years, the three had lived in a rugged lean-to while Tom built a house and furnished it with creations of his hands.

Soon after the Saget family had arrived, the two girls, who were eight years old, had discovered each other. After that, Lacey and Abby had nagged their parents incessantly to be allowed to be together and, under the joy of friendship, the rugged miles between their homes disappeared. Lacey thrilled at every chance to be with Abby and away from the tower. Abby loved to visit the lighthouse, even stay overnight, and, eager to learn alongside her friend, she dutifully copied Lacey's lessons. Her own mother was not as conscientious about schooling her only daughter as Mary Wells was.

But all that was going to change soon for because of what Abby had said and done, nothing would ever be the same between them again.

As Lacey passed through her clearing, she wanted to collapse against a tree trunk and let all the frustration bleed out of her. But she had been away all day and there was always a price to pay for temporary freedom. In the mood she was in, the last thing she wanted to do was endure her mother's

32

scowls if she missed supper. She would have to go home and start peeling potatoes. Quickly and without stopping, she forced herself to cross the clearing. She stormed through the yard, scattering the chickens and rousing the cow from its midafternoon snooze. Her mother had been digging the garden, and Lacey stirred up the loose dirt as she tore through the garden. But she noticed none of the disturbance her return caused and, taking a deep breath, she prepared to enter the realm of decorum required inside the house.

Despite her effort, she let the back door bang behind her as she entered the kitchen. The noise made her mother jump and she turned to examine her daughter's disrrayed countenance. "What has gotten into you?" she asked directly.

"Just having a bad day," Lacey muttered.

"But you've been with Abby, haven't you?"

Lacey nodded.

"You two haven't quarreled in years. I thought you'd outgrown that sort of thing."

"We didn't quarrel." It was true; they had not quarreled. Lacey had held her disappointment until she was out of Abby's sight.

Mary Wells gestured that Lacey should sit down, and she complied. Then she picked up a knife from the table and attacked a potato viciously, knocking a chunk to the floor.

"Lacey!" her mother said. "Just take off the peel, please."

"Sorry."

"Tell me what happened," her mother insisted.

Lacey considered her response. Did her mother really want to know? Would she understand? "Abby's getting married," Lacey blurted out.

Mary Wells raised an eyebrow. "This is cause for such anger? She's eighteen years old and I've always thought she was a sensible girl."

Not like me, though, Lacey thought. *You never thought I was sensible.* Aloud she said, "I think she's making a mistake."

"Is the man a lout or a drunkard?" her mother asked.

"No."

"Is he a believer?"

"Yes, I think so.

"Does he genuinely care for Abby?"

"Yes."

"And she cares for him?"

"Mama, he's a lumberjack!" Lacey knew she would get her mother's sympathy with that fact.

Mary Wells pressed her lips together. "Well, after all, Abby's father is a lumberjack, and he has managed to provide a home for his family. Perhaps this is not a bad thing."

"It's not what she wants. She never wanted to marry a lumberjack. We made a pact that we would never do that."

Mary Wells now seemed amused, which irritated Lacey. "Girlish promises mean nothing in the face of a man's love."

"It wasn't a girlish promise," Lacey muttered. She stabbed an eye out of a potato and held herself from saying more. Her mother had made great sacrifices to come to the peninsula with her father and had endured decades of isolation and harsh living. How could her daughter sit before her and say that she and her best friend had promised each other that they would never settle for what their mothers had done? She kept her mouth shut.

"When is the wedding?" her mother asked.

"In August. She wants me to be her bridesmaid."

"You should be honored."

"She doesn't have any other girlfriends. It's me or nobody."

"Lacey, don't be so harsh. I'm sure she asked you out of genuine affection." Then she changed the subject. "We'll have to talk about this later. Now that you're here to work on supper, I want to give the twins their music lessons." She left the room to find the boys.

Lacey groaned inwardly. Now she would be trapped in the kitchen, listening to Joel and Jeremiah hit every wrong note they could find on the piano. The twins hated their piano lessons, but Mary Wells persisted, as she had with Lacey and

Joshua and no doubt would with Micah.

Lacey decided she had peeled enough potatoes and, reaching to the shelf above the old black stove, she grabbed a big pot and then went out to the water pump in the yard where she could escape a few minutes of torture. Outside, she set the pot under the spout and started to work the handle. The physical effort felt good and she started to calm down as the water began to flow. She pumped harder. When the pot was full, she leaned down to splash her face with the cool water and take in a deep, quieting breath.

"That looks like just what I need," a voice said.

Lacey looked up through the wetness to see sixteen-year-old Joshua approaching. As he strode across the yard toward her, she marveled at how much he looked like a man, not like a little brother. "So the rumor is true," Lacey said, drying her face on her skirt. "You came back."

"I have to come home every few days for a decent meal," Joshua said.

"Mama will never let you come to supper looking like that," Lacey warned.

"I know. Keep pumping." Joshua leaned down and vigorously rubbed water into his face, while his sister pumped.

"Don't lumberjacks believe in bathing?" she asked.

"Too much trouble," Joshua said, chuckling. "I'm hoping Mama will take pity on me and heat enough water to fill the tub."

"She might if you take in a load of wood for the stove."

Joshua rubbed his hands under the last spoutful of water. "I understand you had a visitor here yesterday."

Lacey startled. "Do you mean Travis Gates?"

"He's the one."

"You've met him?"

Joshua shrugged. "Sure. Everybody did. He went around and introduced himself to everyone in the bunkhouse."

"Don't you like him?" Lacey sensed her brother's reserve.

"He's all right. But he doesn't really say much."

"I thought he was quite pleasant." Lacey surprised herself, since she actually shared Joshua's observation.

"Sure, he's pleasant enough," Joshua said, "but something doesn't quite fit. Nobody is sure why he showed up at the camp. It's obvious he's never done this kind of work before."

"He can learn."

"But why would he want to?"

"I thought they were expecting him," Lacey said cautiously.

"Did he tell you that?"

"Well. . .no, not exactly."

"Precisely my point. He doesn't exactly say anything."

"Joshua, don't be ridiculous. You've known him less than twenty-four hours."

Joshua shook his head. "I just don't see how he's going to fit in at the camp."

"Don't jump to conclusions. Give him a chance," Lacey argued, continuing to rise to Travis's defense for reasons she did not understand. "You can't expect to know someone's life history in one day."

"He seemed to know a lot about yours," Joshua said, one corner of his lip turning up, "Letitia."

"Let's change the subject," Lacey said pointedly.

"Okay. Let's talk about Abby. I heard the news. Peter is telling everyone he sees that Abby has agreed to marry him."

Lacey rolled her eyes. Another favorite topic.

"What's the matter?" Joshua asked. "Aren't you happy for Abby? She's your best friend."

"If you want to know the truth, I think she's making a big mistake."

"Now who's jumping to conclusions?" Joshua retorted.

"This is different. I've known Abby more than ten years. Now she'll spend the rest of her life in a log cabin on this peninsula. She never wanted that."

"Peter is going to build her a house, probably as nice a house as her parents have."

"That's what he says. We'll have to see." Lacey was muttering, her irritation renewed.

"Well, I for one think that this is great news. Except for Abby's father, no one else has tried to build a home and raise a family near the camp. Abby and Peter will be pioneers."

"What are you talking about? It's just a lumber camp, and it's as isolated as we are over here."

"Yes, but it doesn't have to be that way forever. We could have a real town on the peninsula. All we need are people willing to build a life and raise their children here. If Peter and Abby do it, some of the other young men will follow."

"Just where are they going to get these wives? I don't see women flocking to the peninsula."

"You're here. That's a start." Joshua grinned.

"You're as crazy as Abby is."

"We're not crazy," Joshua insisted. "Just because you don't want to live here the rest of your life does not mean that it is a bad place to be."

Lacey swallowed and did not respond.

"This peninsula has a future, Lacey. Just wait and see."

Lacey was not convinced. "You'd better go get some clean clothes on. Don't let Mama see you looking like that."

Obediently, and with a parting smile, Joshua turned and went into the house. Lacey slowly picked up the pot, now heavy with water, and followed him.

Mary Wells was in the kitchen now, with the stove growing hot. "There you are," she said. "As soon as the potatoes are done, we'll be ready to eat."

"How did the music lesson go?" Lacey asked, for lack of anything else to say.

"They don't practice nearly enough," her mother responded.

"At least Joshua made it home."

"And he'll stay home for a good while," her mother said insistently. "He's got schoolwork to catch up on."

A thud and a yelp captured their attention. "Joel! Jeremiah!" Mary Wells called out, heading toward the sitting room. "How many times have I told you not to get rough inside the house?"

"Sorry, Mama," came the usual response in unison.

"Go get cleaned up for supper."

The boys shuffled off, snickering about something.

"Will Abby go to the city to get married?" her mother asked while dropping potatoes into the water.

"She wants to get married here," Lacey mumbled.

"But there's no church."

"The minister will come here, and the wedding will be outside."

"The weather should be nice by August." Mary Wells set the lid on the pot.

"I suppose so," Lacey muttered distinterestedly.

"She's only getting married, Lacey. She's not dying, or even moving away."

"I know." Lacey sighed. She should be glad that Abby had found someone who made her happy. But things would never be the same, she was sure of that. All that day Abby had talked of little but Peter, and how much they wanted to have a baby right away. Soon there would be no room in Abby's life for a girlhood friend. Lacey would really be alone then, trapped in the wide open spaces of the peninsula. What pierced her heart most was that at that moment there was not a single person in whom she could confide.

The back door opened and Micah and his father entered. "Just in time," Mary Wells said. "Supper will be ready in ten minutes."

Daniel Wells breathed in the aroma. "Smells delicious."

"Micah, why don't you set the table?" his mother directed.

As he always did, Micah compliantly took the dishes off the shelf and arranged them around the wooden table. Lacey watched his habitual and familiar movements. The family would soon gather for the evening meal, as they always had. Another day had passed, no different from the one before, but nothing would ever be the same for Lacey.

six

"Don't forget that basket on the bench behind you," Mary Wells reminded Lacey as she removed her patched apron and hung it on a nail in the wall.

Lacey, her arms already full, leaned down and looped two fingers through the basket's handle. "This is a lot of food, Mama," she said. For four days her mother had been cooking: three different kinds of bread, spinach puffs, hundreds of meatballs, rice pudding casseroles, and cakes and cookies.

"Today is a celebration," her mother said. "It's Abby's engagement party. She's your friend and her mother is my friend. So, of course, I want to help."

"Will there really be so many people there?" Lacey asked.

"The whole camp, I would imagine. That's more than a hundred people." She glanced at her daughter. "Just wait for your turn. I'll do this and more for your engagement party."

Lacey held her tongue. She hoped that by the time of her engagement she would be faraway from the peninsula. "I'm surprised all the men would be interested in an engagement party," she said.

"Stress the party concept, Lacey," her mother said. "They get to eat something that their cook didn't prepare."

Lacey chuckled. "If Joshua is to be believed, all the men are desperate for real food."

"Papa has the cart ready." Micah burst through the back door with his announcement. "This is going to be so much fun. I can't wait to see the lumber camp."

His mother scowled. "Just remember, we're going there for Abby's party. Don't wander off."

The twins thumped their way down the stairs and into the kitchen and their mother immediately put them to work.

39

"Here, boys, take these crates out to your father."

"I want to ride the horse," Joel said.

"I'm going to do that!" Jeremiah responded emphatically.

"You can take turns," their mother said. "Now go on, load the cart." She handed Joel a crate.

"What about me?" Micah trailed plaintively behind his brothers. "I want a turn."

"The trail's too bumpy. You'll fall off." Jeremiah was leaving no room for argument.

"That's not fair!" Tears sprang to Micah's eyes but, with a basket full of bread in his arms, he followed his brothers out the door.

"I wish there were someplace else to have this party," Mary Wells said, smoothing down her hair. "I hate taking the little boys to the camp."

"The boys are not so little anymore, Mama," Lacey said.

"I just don't want them getting any ideas, that's all."

"You always let me go see Abby."

"That was different. I didn't have to worry that you would decide to be a lumberjack."

Lacey held her tongue. She knew her mother disapproved of Joshua's choice to work in the camp.

"We'd better get going." Mary Wells nudged her daughter and both of them, loaded with baskets and platters, joined the rest of the family in the yard.

The weeks since Abby had announced her engagement had brought vibrant, warm weather and Mary Wells's vegetables sprouted through the black earth in perfect straight rows. Daniel took over loading the small wooden cart that their one horse would pull, wedging each item securely enough to survive the ride intact.

"Are you going to ride in the cart, Micah?" he asked.

The boy's bottom lip was hanging out. "I want to ride the horse," he muttered.

Daniel Wells glanced at the twins, already grabbing at the reins; the old mare seemed disinterested in the process.

"Maybe we can work something out on the way home. If you change your mind about the cart, let me know."

They started out, heading across the property to the edge of the woods. Joel was on the mare while Jeremiah trotted alongside, complaining. Daniel Wells made a good-natured attempt to distract Micah, and Mary Wells and Lacey walked side by side at the rear of the caravan, each absorbed in her own thoughts.

Finally, the miles were behind them and they emerged from the forest into the small dirt street that ran the length of the camp. Buildings erected two decades ago in a makeshift effort still stood, giving shelter for cooking and sleeping. A rickety stable housed a dozen horses used to haul logs. The only substantive structures were the common hall where the lumberjacks ate their morning and evening meals and the house where Abby's family lived. The house was at the end of the street, set well back from the flow of traffic around it and isolated by a large lawn that Abby's father tended faithfully over the years.

Abby and Peter stood holding hands in the yard in front of the house and Lacey stood down the street and watched them as they greeted their guests. Reluctantly, she had to admit that they looked happy. Gone was the wistful expression that her friend had carried for years. In its place was a relaxed smile that Lacey envied. Abby may have compromised her youthful ambitions, but at least now she knew what her future was.

Lacey started toward them to offer her congratulations but her eyes fastened on the couple as she saw Travis Gates approach them. He slapped Peter on the back and shook his hand heartily. Resting his hands on his hips, he seemed content to stand and chat for a few minutes. Lacey hesitated, but Abby had spotted Lacey and was waving for her to join them. Lacey put a smile on her face and moved more quickly.

"Travis tells me he's already met your family," Abby said. She smiled at Travis as she squeezed Peter's hand. "He and Peter have become great friends."

"Oh? That's nice," Lacey said. "Hello, Travis. I'm glad to see you again."

"And I'm delighted to see you, too."

"Maybe the four of us could spend some time together," Abby gushed.

Lacey caught herself before gasping out loud.

Travis came to the rescue. "Are your brothers here, too?"

Lacey nodded. "The three youngest are beside themselves. They love to come here."

"Having been here for a few weeks, I can see why boys would find it exciting." Travis glanced around. "Something tells me the twins are all right on their own. But would your mother mind if I gave Micah a tour?"

Lacey tilted her head in the direction she had come from. "He's back over there. . .and I'm sure he'd rather be with you than with Mama."

"I'll go with you," Peter said. "I'd like to say hello to Lacey's mother."

The men left and Abby turned to Lacey. "I'm so glad you came, Lacey."

"Why wouldn't I come?"

"Something tells me you're not keen on my marrying Peter."

"Don't be ridiculous. I want you to be happy," Lacey said sincerely. "If marrying Peter will make you happy, then of course I'm happy for you."

"Thanks. You're the only real friend I had growing up. I know we always said we were going to get away from here, so you must think I'm crazy for staying. But Peter and I are going to make a life here, and we'll have lots of children. I'm going to teach them all the way your mother taught all of you." Abby glanced up toward Peter and Travis as they walked away. "Peter likes Travis a lot. He's going to ask him to help build our house."

Lacey raised an eyebrow. "I thought Travis was only here temporarily."

"He's not sure when he's leaving," Abby said. "I hope he'll stay a long time. And I hope you'll get a chance to get to know him."

Lacey did not respond. Abby had verbalized what she secretly hoped but dared not say.

"Oh, look! The string band is starting to play." Abby pointed across the street.

"Where did you get a band?" Lacey asked in astonishment.

"Anything is possible when my mother puts her mind to it," Abby answered.

"The food tables look incredible," Lacey added. "When our two mothers put their minds together, there is sure to be enough to feed the multitudes. Let's go get something to eat."

Abby put her hand on her waist. "I'm so excited that I don't think I could eat anything."

Lacey pulled on her friend's elbow. "Oh, come on. It's your engagement party. You have to at least try. My mother made those spinach puffs you like."

Abby followed reluctantly as Lacey retraced her steps to where she had left her mother setting up food.

"Mrs. Wells, everything looks wonderful!" Abby exclaimed. Her fingers traced the edge of a meat platter.

Mary Wells gave a satisfied smile. "As soon as your father gives the signal, everyone can start eating."

Abby rolled her eyes. "I hope he's not going to make one of his speeches."

Lacey laughed. "Of course, he will. That's what fathers do at moments like this."

"Come with me, Abby," Mary Wells said. "Let's find your father."

"Lacey!" Micah's shrill cry took her by surprise.

"Micah! What is it?" He flew into his sister's arms.

"Travis is showing me everything. I got to see the big saws! And where they put the logs in the water to float them to the mill!"

"Even Joshua didn't get to do that until he was ten!" Lacey joined her brother's delight. She raised her eyes to see Travis, coming up behind Micah. "You've made my brother really happy."

Travis grinned. "It was my pleasure, I assure you. There is no one else around to show off my newly found knowledge to."

Lacey laughed. "From what I hear, you're getting to be an old hand around here."

Travis set his hands on his hips, a gesture Lacey had noticed several times. He exuded contentment.

"Abby says you and Peter have become friends," Lacey said.

Travis nodded. "He's a thinker, that Peter. He has big plans."

Lacey was not sure what to say. She had known Peter slightly for several years and had never seen him in this light.

Micah was tugging on Travis's arm. "Come on, show me more."

"Be patient," Lacey chastised gently.

Travis smoothed the boy's hair. "I have a lot more to show you. Why don't you meet me in front of the band in a few minutes."

"I'll be there! But don't take too long." Micah shot off directly for the string band.

Travis turned to Lacey. "This is a party, with a hundred things going on, but I'm glad I got to see you."

"Likewise," Lacey blushed.

"How do you spend your Sundays?"

"Oh, I. . . Well, there's no church, you know, so we just. . . Well, it's pretty much a regular day."

"Well, everyone in the camp has Sundays off," Travis said. "I'd like to come and see you. Would that be all right?"

Lacey swallowed, hardly believing her ears. "I'd like that," she said. "How about a picnic? We could eat in the clearing where the path comes out."

"Perfect. I'll look for you there about two o'clock."

"Travis!" Micah's soprano voice somehow carried over the growing noise of the crowd.

"Gotta go," Travis said with a quick smile.

Lacey turned around and nervously rearranged the food trays. Once she glanced over her shoulder to see Travis drape his hand around Micah's shoulders.

From his vantage point across the street, Travis could not tell that her efforts were needless. He simply admired her slim form and the thoughtful tilt of her head as the sun burnished golden highlights in the hair falling around her shoulders.

"My sister is really nice," Micah said. "Do you like her?"

Travis looked down at the boy, wondering how much those blue eyes understood. "Yes, Micah, I like your sister."

seven

Meeting Travis in the clearing on Sunday afternoons quickly became a habit, and one that Lacey welcomed. Knowing that she could look forward to his companionship on the weekends made the drudgery of the week more bearable. She found herself plunging into laundry and cooking and gardening without the usual exhortations from her mother. She even nagged at the twins to be more helpful, pleading the cause of their mother's enormous workload. As she tended the vegetables that year, pressing the seeds into the dark soil and pulling weeds, she looked forward to their sprouting and sprawling all over the plot, rather than dreading the fact that she would still be there to see the late-summer harvest that would carry the family through another winter.

Lacey hardly noticed when spring blended into summer and, before she knew it, the grass in the meadow was knee high and Micah was spending his afternoons there while the mare and the cow grazed. He had started a butterfly collection and Lacey laughed riotously as she watched him chase the colorful flutters with his homemade net. Miraculously, he caught several.

By the time the hot days of July were upon them, Lacey and Travis were used to each other and content to indulge in extended speculation about life on the peninsula and life in a real town. Lacey liked best the times that Travis wandered through his memories and described the town he had grown up in with its school, a church, neighbors, and shops—all the things Lacey had hungered for as a child, and still did.

The first few times they agreed to meet, Lacey was not sure Travis would come. She imagined dozens of reasons that would keep him away, not the least of which was her own personality.

She longed to pour out her feelings to someone who had lived somewhere else and might understand her drive to find a life away from the peninsula. But Travis had chosen to come to the peninsula, though Lacey never quite understood why, and she did not want to drive him away with chronic complaining.

Her brothers, of course, taunted her mercilessly. Joel called her picnic basket the "love basket." Not to be outdone, Jeremiah kept a running log of "the love food" that she put in it each week. Micah won coveted approval from the twins for his part in the onslaught. Naturally, they did all this behind their mother's back, and Lacey was much too old to go sniveling to her mother to make them stop. At first she had been infuriated and demanded that they mind their own business but this sent them howling into mimicry and only made the situation worse. Eventually, Lacey steeled herself to ignore them and she managed to hold her tongue.

Even her mother took a different attitude toward her. Wordlessly, she made sure Sunday afternoons were free of activities that would tie Lacey down. And when Micah chattered on about his fascination with Travis, she looked over her son's blond head at her daughter's brown-haired one, her faced covered with a knowing look and a vague smile.

In between Sundays, Lacey made her habitual visits to the clearing alone for it was still her escape, the place where she could let her thoughts run free and close her eyes and dream of another place. Also, Travis's presence lingered in that place, drawing Lacey to it even more than ever.

Every week, when Travis arrived at the clearing, she relived their first meeting there. She had snuck out of the house with the prettiest quilt handed down to her from her grandmother, and she had reached the clearing early. Cold chicken, chocolate cake, and a jug of sweetened lemonade comprised the picnic lunch that she spread out on the quilt and then waited. Without a clock nearby, she was not sure how much time had passed, but it seemed like far too much. Travis had realized his folly and changed his mind, she had told herself. So she might as well pack up and go home.

But, just as she was convinced that Travis was not going to come, he had emerged from the woods, paused at the edge of the path, and smiled at her. The sun was in front of him, throwing a magical golden glow across his tanned face. Lacey lurched to her feet to greet him, nearly kicking over the basket of chicken.

"Hello," he said simply.

"Hello," she answered, and their friendship had begun.

The day came when Mary Wells suggested that it was time that Lacey should bring Travis home for dinner one Sunday afternoon. Inwardly she resisted. When she was with Travis, she was in a world of fresh perspectives, dreams, and a vision of the future. To take Travis home for dinner would taint her new world.

But she knew it had to be done, and so she had done it. The twins snickered and Micah climbed all over Travis. Mary Wells kept the food coming while managing not to miss a word of the conversation between her husband and the handsome young man. Lacey said little that day and breathed a sigh of relief when she and Travis finally broke away for a walk.

In the weeks that followed, Abby pleaded that she needed Lacey's help to prepare for her wedding and Lacey gladly took advantage of this as an excuse for frequent trips across the peninsula. They stitched beads on a gown made of white silk that Abby's mother had been saving for years for just this occasion.

In the past, Lacey had not paid much attention to news about the camp or the lumber business, but now her ears perked up when Abby mentioned these things. According to Abby, Peter raved about Travis Gates.

"What does he say?" Lacey asked.

"Travis is a fast learner, and strong. He can handle the saws as well as men who have been there for years."

Lacey thought about how she had noticed his soft hands

becoming calloused and rough. How his hands must have hurt in the first few weeks, yet he never complained.

"Peter says everybody likes him," Abby continued. "Usually the new men have to prove themselves, and they get the worst jobs, the heaviest loads, the most danger. It's a test, to see if they can make it as lumberjacks. Travis has never let anyone down." Abby looked slyly at her friend. "But of course you know that, don't you?"

Lacey blushed. Abby knew that she was seeing Travis every week, but Lacey guarded against divulging too many details of their conversations.

During one session to work on the dress, Abby stood on a stool wearing the gown while Lacey, on her knees, pinned the hem in place. "There he is," Abby said suddenly.

"Who?" Lacey mumbled through the pins in her mouth.

"Travis. He just passed by the window. I think he's coming to the door," Abby said.

A few seconds later, they heard his solid rap.

"It's open! Come on in," Abby called.

The door swung in and Travis poked his head around it. Lacey spat pins into one hand.

"Hello," she said.

He smiled. "I didn't know you would be here. I would have cleaned up."

"You look great." To her own surprise, Lacey meant what she said. His face gleamed with sweat, and his shirt was smudged with layers of sap and mud. She could see he was being careful not to touch anything with his dirty hands. Never before had a grimy lumberjack looked so appealing to her. He was looking for Tom Saget and, after having gathered Abby's opinions about where he might be, Travis was on his way.

"See, it can happen," Abby said.

"What do you mean?"

"It is possible to fall in love with a lumberjack."

Lacey stuck a pin through the hem, hitting Abby's ankle.

"Ouch!" Abby cried.

"Sorry," Lacey said.

"You don't have to stick me with a pin just because I can see what's happening between you and Travis."

"Regardless of what may or may not be happening between us, Travis is not a lumberjack."

"He works in a lumber camp."

"It's temporary. He said from the start that he would only be here a few months."

Abby shrugged. "It doesn't look to me like he's in any hurry to leave."

Lacey bit back her response for Abby had touched on the one thing that troubled her about Travis. It did seem like he was settling into life on the peninsula rather well. When he first arrived, she had thought he was a breath of fresh air, but if he stayed too long. . .she hated to think what might happen. She had grown attached to Travis, yes, but not enough to be content with the peninsula.

There was a day not too long ago when Lacey realized that her relationship with Travis had taken a new turn. They had been walking in the woods after eating, and she had pointed out the complexity of the wildlife existing along the edge of the trail: small rodents burrowing into the ground; birds nesting in the high branches; ants marching out in force in search of food; tiny bugs clinging to the wildflower petals. They had bent over a blue wildflower, daring not to breathe on it lest the object of their fascination flitter away. With their heads bent low, close together, Lacey could feel his breath on her neck. When they stood up, he had taken her face in his hands to kiss it, and she did not resist. In fact, she had hoped for weeks that this moment would come.

She had indeed fallen in love with Travis Gates. But could she love a lumberjack?

She shuddered at the thought of it. Travis had not said anything to her about staying on the peninsula, and she refused to believe he would. And, when he did leave, she sincerely hoped he would take her with him.

eight

Sullen gray clouds clumped in the western sky, readying for a summer thunderstorm. Wind blew through Lacey's hair as she studied the formation, and she pressed her hand to the back of her neck to keep her hair under control. The clouds were the sort that could produce a quick shower and pass by or barrage the peninsula for hours. Her father, she knew, would know the difference. His weather watching habits had spanned the five decades of his life. Each day he carefully logged signs of change and later noted what had resulted.

Lacey stood on the lighthouse balcony, looking out over the passageway. This was the best time of year for boats to navigate the passage, and even as a child, Lacey had loved to come to the balcony and watch for boats. She would make up stories about the people on them, stories of adventure, daring, and romance in faraway places.

Sometimes, standing on the balcony high above the water and scanning the horizon, she felt as if she were at the edge of the world. She knew she ought to step back from the edge, step back to safety, yet she wanted to lean farther over the railing. What was over the edge? Was there a whole new world she could not see from where she was?

Lacey took her eyes off the clouds and glanced at the water. A boat was coming; it was Gordon Wright's supply boat, right on schedule. Gordon knew the rocks of the passageway better than anyone else who sailed through. Lacey watched now as he swung the wooden vessel around a curve and straightened its path toward the Wells family's dock below. Joshua and the twins were taking their places, and her mother had come out of the house with a crumpled list in her hand.

51

Her father tousled Micah's hair and smiled at his enthusiasm. It was all so predictable, Lacey thought. It was just a rickety boat with its rude owner bringing them the bare necessities for their survival in this place. Why was that worthy of celebration every few weeks?

Daniel Wells cupped his hands around his mouth and called up to his daughter. Although his words were carried away on the wind and she heard only drifting tenor tones, Lacey knew he was summoning her to come down and take her place in the drama. This time Joshua was there to help with the heavy work, so Lacey would help her mother put the food and household supplies in their proper places.

Reluctantly she pulled herself away from the railing and turned to find the small door to the spiral iron staircase when a patch of red flashed to one side, and she automatically raised her eyes. The red was a shirt, a lumberjack's shirt, but not Joshua's and, to her delight, she saw that Travis and Peter were in the meadow. Peter patted the rump of a horse and left it to graze. Lacey scrunched up her face in a puzzle. What were they doing here in the middle of a workday at a busy time of the lumber year? Instinctively she raked her fingers through her windblown hair, wishing she had taken the time to tie it back properly that morning. But windblown or not, she was glad to see Travis and now felt no reluctance to descend from the edge of the world.

She reached the bottom of the stairs and pushed open the door. She squinted for a moment, for even the dull afternoon was brighter than the dank stairwell inside the tower. She saw that Peter and Travis had reached the edge of the garden. Ignoring the twins who were calling her, she walked toward the visitors instead and, when they were near each other, she pivoted and fell into step with them.

"Hello, Lacey," Peter said. He reached into his pocket for an envelope. "Abby sent this."

"Oh. Thank you." She stuck the note in the pocket of her skirt to read later and smiled at Travis, awaiting his greeting.

"Is Gordon here yet?" Travis asked, glancing toward the dock.

"Gordon? He's just about to dock."

"Good. Excuse me. Peter, I'll catch up with you later." With a wordless glance at Lacey, Travis quickened his step and trotted ahead of them.

Lacey's steps slowed as she scowled. "What was that all about?"

"He's expecting some important mail. He's hoping Gordon will have it."

"Does that mean he can't even say hello?" Lacey heard the sharpness in her own voice. "Joshua would have taken the mail when he goes back to the camp tomorrow."

Peter shrugged. "I'm not sure what's going on."

"And what brings you here?"

Peter grinned. "Abby's father sent me. They're expecting some fancy things for the wedding. City stuff."

"Oh."

They continued walking toward the edge of the cliff. By the time they reached it, Travis was winding the pulley with the first load; the twins were glad to be relieved of the effort. As the barrel tipped over the top of the pulley, Joshua pushed it off onto the ground. Under their mother's supervision, Joel and Jeremiah started rolling it toward the house. Micah squirmed in under Travis's chest to help with the crank.

"Where's my Lacey?" Gordon called out.

Lacey rolled her eyes and then glanced at Travis for his reaction. He had none; he just cranked.

"Lacey Wells, come and say hello!" Gordon insisted.

She craned her neck to see him. "Hello, Gordon. How are you?"

"Not as well as I would be if you could take a boat ride with me."

"Not today, Gordon," she said flatly, as usual.

"I'll be asking again. You know I will."

Peter chuckled beside her. "He never gives up, does he? I

wonder if he knows about you and Travis."

Lacey thought to herself, *And I wonder what there is to know.*

The next load up had a small canvas pouch tucked between the ropes. It was the mailbag and Travis plucked it off the crate before anyone else could reach it. Glancing over his shoulder, he said, "Hey, Pete, put yourself to work over here." Then he turned and walked away from the crank, unfastening the buckle on the mailbag as he went.

Mystified, Lacey watched as Travis sat on a boulder across the yard and started flipping through the letters in the bag. Finally, he pulled one out and held it in his hand. He glanced at her for a fraction of a second, then pulled his eyes away.

꙳

What will she think? Travis wondered. *Have I gone too far?*

Mary Wells called for Lacey and she turned to help her mother. Travis watched her movements: competent, smooth, efficient. But he knew she cared little about what she was doing. She always urged him to talk about where he had come from, as if she could sit for hours and listen to stories about life in a real town. Would she ever know contentment, here or anywhere else?

He tore off the end of the envelope and slid out the papers. They were exactly what he was hoping for.

"Hey, Travis!" Micah called, running toward him. "Did you know Peter is even stronger than you are? He's turning the pulley fast!"

Travis smiled and held out his hand to the boy, who perched next to him on the rock. "Peter has been working outside for a long time. He's used to the hard work."

꙳

Looking up from her work, Lacey saw Travis chatting with Micah. That was one of the things she liked most about Travis: his willingness to take his time with Micah. She watched as he folded up his letter and tucked it in his shirt pocket. *What was that all about? What could possibly be that urgent?* He once mentioned that he had almost been engaged to a girl in his hometown and that they were still friends. *What did that mean? Are they sending letters back and forth? That might explain why he had practically ignored me earlier.*

"I'll be right back, Mama," she said, having decided to approach Travis again, this time with Micah as a buffer. Resisting the temptation to gather her skirt in one hand and run toward the rock, she walked casually with her hands in her pockets. She felt Abby's note waiting for her attention.

"Hello," she said lightly. "I hope Micah is not disturbing you."

"No, of course not," Travis replied. Lacey thought his voice sounded strained. "But I suppose I'd better get back to work soon or Peter will tell tales on me."

"I'll help!" Micah's enthusiasm never waned.

"Great. I'll tell you what. You go over and see what's going on, and I'll meet you in a few minutes." Travis glanced up at Lacey.

"Oh. You want to talk to my sister," Micah guessed.

Travis laughed and Lacey felt awkward. "I can't fool you, can I?" Travis said.

"Don't take too long." Micah scurried over to help Joel and Jeremiah roll kerosene barrels.

"Hello." The long-awaited greeting came.

"Hello," she responded.

"Micah's right. I did want to talk to you about something." Travis gestured that she should sit down.

Lacey swallowed involuntarily for she was hearing a tone in his voice she had not heard before.

He slid the envelope out of his pocket. "I've been waiting for this to come," he said. "It's addressed to me, but actually it's for you."

Puzzled, she took the envelope from his hand, extracted the paper, and read the letter.

Dear Mr. Gates,

*Thank you for inquiring about the teaching position on
behalf of your friend, Miss Wells. We would be happy to
consider her application. From what you have said, I am
sure she would have no difficulty passing the qualifying
examination.*

Lacey absorbed very little after that. "Teaching position?"
she said, incredulous.

Travis nodded. "I haven't said anything to you, because I
wasn't sure it was my place. But. . .well, we have become
friends, and I care about your feelings. I thought. . .perhaps you
would be happy to have an opportunity to leave the peninsula,
at least for a time."

"But, Travis, teaching? I don't know." She swallowed her
true thoughts. *Yes, I want to leave but not alone.*

"I think you would be good at it. From what I've seen, your
mother has done a better job than most organized schools in
educating you and your brothers. The twins get on your nerves,
they're at an awkward age, but I see the way you are with
Micah. Imagine the effect you could have on a whole class of
children like him."

"But I've never even considered being a teacher! I wouldn't
know where to begin."

Travis paused and lowered his eyes. "I know you're not
happy here, Lacey, but when I try to picture what would make
you happy, I can't quite fill in all the colors. After a while, I
realized that no one can do that for you and that you have to do
it yourself. I do know that God has given you some wonderful
gifts, and you should find a way to use them."

Lacey swallowed hard. "But, Travis—"

"The teaching position is for only nine months," Travis continued, "because the regular teacher has to be away. But she's
coming back. They're just looking for someone to fill in."

"How did you know about this job?"

"A friend of my father mentioned it in a letter, and I wrote for more information." Travis reached for Lacey's hand. "I kept wanting to say something but I wasn't sure how you would react."

"I am not sure what to say. You've gone to all this trouble. I suppose I should be grateful." Confusion overwhelmed her.

"It's for only nine months. If you hate it, then you'll know teaching is not for you. But you might love it!"

"Where is the school?" Lacey asked. Her mother, she knew, would ask sensible questions.

"South. It's not a big place," Travis explained, "not the city that you would prefer. But after you get some teaching experience, you could apply for a better job somewhere else."

"It doesn't matter how small the town might be. It's sure to be bigger than here."

Travis smiled. "You're seeing the advantages already."

Lacey focused her eyes on a mushroom at her feet. "Are you leaving the peninsula, Travis?"

"I don't know. I came here because I felt led to come here."

"Led? By God?"

He nodded. "And I'll stay until it's time to leave. In the meantime, I'm content. I just want you to be content, too. You have to make your own decision, find your sense of call."

"I don't know what to say, Travis." Her voice was low but her heart was screaming, *I thought you would take me away from here, not send me away!*

"Just think about it, Lacey. But they need an answer soon because the job starts in two months."

"Gates! Go get the horse and help me with this stuff!" Peter held a large canvas bag in his arms, and another lay at his feet.

Questioning, Travis looked at Lacey and drew her eyes up to meet his.

Silently, she nodded.

nine

The train slowed. Being careful to keep her hat on straight, Lacey pressed her face as close to the window as she dared. The blur of golden trees gradually gave form to trunks and limbs embellished with burnished leaves. Carefully painted wooden homes stopped spinning and announced that the train had arrived in a town. Abruptly, the train lurched to a stop and the whistle blew. Lacey's stomach flipped with uncertainty about the commitment she had made.

Travis had not proposed. Instead, he had found Lacey a job. He was giving her what she had said she wanted: a reason to leave the peninsula with which even her mother could not argue. Lacey was going to be a teacher for the next nine months, and it was her mother who had prepared her so well for this role.

But was she truly prepared? Lacey wondered. Yes, she had always been a good student and now she even helped her mother with lessons for the twins and Micah. But that was very different from a whole classroom of children she did not know. She had passed the qualifying test with one of the highest scores ever seen, but did that make her a teacher?

Around her, the other passengers were gathering their things and leaving the train. Now Lacey did the same. She had not brought much for she did not have much to bring. Her hand-me-down trunk was in the baggage car, and she had only a small bag of essentials, which she now grasped tightly. Smoothing her skirt and wrapping her coat tightly as she walked, Lacey made her way down the aisle to the door at the back of the train car. Now she could get her first real look at this new town.

Outside the train, Lacey scanned the station. Most of the

people on the train had gotten off at this stop and the platform bustled with confusion and greetings. A few feet from Lacey, a young wife with three children in tow greeted her husband with a kiss. Down the platform, a businessman dressed in a shiny black suit barked orders at his junior companion. Lacey got bumped from the back by a thin, teenage boy lumbering along the platform with his mother's trunk.

Where was Maria Johnson? Lacey wondered about her teaching partner who was supposed to meet her. But Lacey did not even know what Maria looked like.

"You look lost," said a voice behind Lacey.

Lacey spun around, grasping for words, as she faced a stout woman, perhaps ten years older than herself. "I. . .I'm to be met here, I think."

"I know. I'm meeting you," said the woman.

"Miss Johnson?" Lacey asked, hope rising within her.

"Maria," came the reply. "You match the description perfectly."

"Description?"

"Yes, the chairman of the school board gave me a written description. When did you meet him?" Maria turned and started to walk down the platform.

"I haven't," Lacey said. *Travis*, she thought. *Travis must have written the description.*

"He seems to know all about you," Maria said. "I have a wagon hitched up to the horse. Let's find your trunk." She walked toward the baggage car that was already unloaded, the trunks and bags heaped on the platform.

"There it is," Lacey said as she pointed at the the faded green metal trunk that her mother had brought to the peninsula as a bride more than twenty years ago.

"Wouldn't you know, it's at the bottom of the pile," Maria grumbled. "I'll just have a word with a porter." Briskly Maria marched down the platform in pursuit of a porter.

It was not long before the trunk was extricated from the heap and loaded onto the waiting wagon. Maria gestured that

Lacey should climb onto the bench at the front of the wagon, behind the horse. From the other side, Maria heaved herself up and picked up the reins.

"Ready?" Maria asked.

"Ready," Lacey answered softly, even though she was not sure she was.

The horse trotted down the street, the wagon rattling behind. By usual standards, the town was not large but to Lacey it seemed enormous. A row of shops nearly made her burst out like a child, and the steeple of a church convinced her she was going to like this town. A few houses were clustered in neat rows, just like a real neighborhood! Gradually, the houses were spaced farther and farther apart. Now they were headed out on an open dirt road. Confused, Lacey could not contain her questions.

"Aren't we headed out of town now?" she asked.

Maria nodded. "We're leaving Paxton. That's just where the train comes in."

"Oh," Lacey said.

Maria turned to look at Lacey. "Did you think that was Tyler Creek?"

Now Lacey was more confused. "What's Tyler Creek?"

"The town where you will be teaching? Didn't they tell you anything?"

"They told me to take the train to Paxton, and that you would meet me there."

Maria threw her head back and laughed. "No doubt they were afraid you would change your mind if you knew the truth about Tyler Creek."

Lacey's stomach was in a knot now. "Please tell me what you are talking about."

"Tyler Creek is a small, small community about five miles from here. That's where the school is."

"Small?"

"We have about six hundred people," Maria explained. "A few have small shops, more are farmers or millworkers."

"Six hundred people?" Lacey echoed.

"I know that doesn't sound like many people to folks who live in the city."

"To me, six hundred is a city!" In her mind, Lacey added up the lumberjacks who made up the population of the peninsula; perhaps a hundred, she thought. "What is the school like?"

"Not all of the children come to school," Maria explained. "We have an enrollment of about fifty, split into two classes."

"And I'll have the lower grades?"

Maria nodded. "That's what Victoria was teaching before she had to go on leave."

Lacey's curiosity got the best of her. "Why did she have to leave?"

Maria's jaw stiffened and her face clouded over. "She became ill, and her family thought it best that she go home for a time of rest."

"Ill?"

But Maria said no more.

"Is there a mercantile in Tyler Creek," Lacey asked, changing the subject.

Maria's smile returned. "No, no mercantile. But there is Mister Edgars who comes around every few weeks with his truck loaded down with everything a body could want."

"What about food?"

Maria gestured widely. "Look around. This is farm country. Folks grow what they need."

"But you don't farm," Lacey pointed out.

"No, just a few vegetables. But I never lack for food. And neither will you. I'd wager that we'll send you home a good twenty pounds heavier."

Lacey put her hand on her slender waist. "I hope not!" She shivered and crossed her arms to hug herself. "I hadn't expected it to be so cool in September. My home is so far north. I thought it would be better down here."

"This is still Wisconsin," Maria reminded Lacey. "And winter is not far off. We don't have too much farther to go."

At last the horse lumbered into a small gathering of houses and the animal seemed to know where he was going without further prodding. He turned left off the main road and trotted lazily down a dirt path.

"Here we are," Maria said finally, pulling on the reins gently. "Home, sweet home."

Maria jumped down and unhitched the horse. Lacey moved more slowly, inspecting her surroundings at the same time that she found the ground under her feet again. Before her was a small house, just a cottage. No doubt, its clapboard had once been a shiny white, but now it was dull gray and chipped. The three steps leading up to the front door sagged precariously.

Lacey turned slightly to see what Maria was doing. It was then she noticed the small building separated from the cottage by a small yard. A well-beaten path led directly from the cottage steps to the other building. The school, Lacey surmised.

"Do you want to take the trunk in now, or get cleaned up first?" Lacey had already figured out that Maria was a practical soul.

"Let's do it now," Lacey mumbled. Without the help of a porter, managing the trunk would be much more difficult than earlier.

Maria heaved the trunk down off the back of the wagon and dirt sprayed as it hit the ground. Lacey winced, glad she had not brought anything breakable.

"You've got more than clothes in here," Maria announced.

"Books," Lacey confessed. "I wasn't sure what there would be here."

Maria nodded knowingly. "You did the wise thing."

"Let me help you with that."

Together they carried the trunk into the house. Lacey glanced around the sitting room as they passed through. An overstuffed chair and a well-worn table were the predominant features, arranged on a faded braided rug that had once been a rich green.

"This is your room." With one hand, Maria pushed open a

door. They set the trunk down with care on the bare wooden floor. "I'm going to put the kettle on while you settle in."

Lacey's room was not much bigger than her room at home. The bed swung low to the floor and the iron headboard needed a fresh coat of paint. Sheets and a patchwork quilt were neatly folded at the foot of the bare mattress. A small dresser was wedged under the window. Four pegs in the wall would serve as a closet. Lacey slowly opened her trunk and considered how to arrange her things. The options were few and the task was soon complete.

Lacey went out to the sitting room that she would share with Maria. Her new roommate stirred up the fire in the old black stove, and then she wiped her hands on a dingy apron.

"This is for heat and for cooking," Maria explained. "It's not fancy, but nothing in Tyler Creek is fancy."

No, it's not fancy, Lacey thought silently, *but it's not the peninsula. I said I wanted to leave and I have.*

"Are you hungry?" Maria moved toward the nook of a kitchen. "I'll fix you some bread and tea."

Lacey nodded gratefully. *Father, keep me thankful*, she prayed silently as her heart raced slightly, *and show me what it is I am here to do.*

ten

Lacey struck a solid chord on the decrepit spinet with a cracked top that was at the back of her classroom. The tinny clang made her wince for the instrument was badly out of tune and at least a dozen strings were missing. Sometimes she wondered why she bothered to try to teach music with that piano, but it was all she had. According to Maria, no one had taught music to the children in more than seven years. Lacey was determined to change that, but the idea of an a cappella choir appealed more every day. But she was committed to the piano for now.

Winterfest would begin the next day and Tyler Creek, as tiny as it was, would gather all its citizens to celebrate that winter was nearly over. Soon, they would have some relief from pelting sleet and howling wind, but slick, icy roads would turn to mud, which would no doubt mean broken buggy axles and chronically sloppy floors.

The fall weeks had blurred together as Lacey had sorted out the task before her. Lacey's first day in the classroom had been a mixture of terror and delight. Helping her mother give lessons to Micah and the twins was one thing; facing a roomful of children ranging in age from four to ten years old was something else entirely. She had stood before them, immobilized. The little ones in the front turned their faces up expectantly. In the back of the room, two older boys leaned toward each other and muttered, looking at her suspiciously all the while. In Lacey's mind the words were flowing, but somehow they did not seem to come out of her mouth. At last a little girl named Sally had asked, "Are you all right, Miss Wells?" and Lacey had snapped herself together and gone into action.

Lacey had learned from her mother to stay in control at

lesson time and the shenanigans of her twin brothers had prepared her for what she faced now. The muttering boys in the back were gently but firmly reprimanded, and class had begun.

It took nearly two weeks for Lacey to assess every student's abilities and discern their temperaments. She knew that the students in her class would be as different from each other as Micah was from Joel and Jeremiah. Yet, they all had to learn to read and do basic figuring. And Lacey wanted to add music, geography, and art to the curriculum. She was not teaching one class; she was teaching several classes. Dalton and Denys, the two biggest boys were old enough to be in Maria's class. But they had missed too many days of school in the last two years and they did not read well enough to move on to the next class. Lacey's dilemma was that she was not sure they wanted to learn to read and that they might very well spend yet another year in the same classroom.

At the other end of the spectrum was a child who was not even five years old but who insisted on going to school with his older siblings, and his mother had allowed it. Little Jonathan was well-behaved and was really no trouble, but Lacey did not feel she could extend the curriculum to such a young age and so she was not sure what he was learning.

At the end of each day, Lacey gathered papers and books and scurried across the clearing between the school and the cottage. It was too cold to be outside and everywhere she went, she went quickly. With Maria, she huddled around the blackened stove they used for both heat and cooking. The evenings were crammed with lesson planning. The previous teacher had left some notes and outlines, but most of her scribblings were not meaningful to Lacey so she had to start over from the beginning. Maria was some help, although most of her experience was with the older children. Night after night, Lacey sat up late with a candle, a wool shawl wrapped around her shoulders, planning lessons that would teach Roger how to add double figures and Bessie to sound out the words on the page. She had to find a way to make Wiley pay attention and stop looking out the window. And TJ simply needed encouragement that he could succeed at school.

Books were in shockingly short supply and three children shared one copy of a basic textbook. Victoria had left behind a few storybooks, and Lacey added some of her own to the meager collection. Maria had scowled when Lacey announced she was going to let the children borrow the books and take them home to read. It was a risk that some of the books would never make it back, but Lacey was compelled to act on her conviction that children must be stimulated with new ideas and experiences. She found it difficult to believe that even tucked away on a distant peninsula, she had grown up with more books than many of these children would ever hold. She had begun to see her own mother in a new light.

Christmastime had come and Lacey had remained in Tyler Creek. A couple of times she took the wagon into Paxton where the festive spirit was more evident. An array of sugary cakes and candles made Lacey pine to be with her family. But that was not possible. There would be other years, she told herself, to savor her mother's roast duck on Christmas Eve and to tie bows to the window panes.

On Christmas Eve she went to the midnight service at the small church in Tyler Creek. While singing the carols, for the first time with more people than her immediate family, her heart surged to receive anew the gift God freely offered.

After Christmas, the weather took a severe turn. School was shut down several times and families huddled at their hearths, but Winterfest would bring them out and Lacey wanted the children to be ready.

Children bustled around her, jostling each other for a space in the front row. They had worked hard already that afternoon, and Lacey knew she would not have their attention for much longer.

She struck the chord again, raising and lowering her hands

to the keys four times. "Children, children," she said, "we're almost through."

Maria had raised her eyebrows at Lacey's idea that a children's choir should sing at Winterfest but Lacey was determined, and for the most part, the children were enthusiastic, if not attentive.

"How can we practice without TJ?" a thin voice asked. Rebekah looked at her teacher, wondering.

Lacey sighed. It was a legitimate question. TJ had the solo part in the last song. This was the final rehearsal before the performance, and TJ was nowhere to be found. He had not been in school for two days.

"I suppose we can't wait for him any longer," Lacey conceded. "He learned the part so well, and he has such a beautiful voice. Are you sure none of you knows where he is?" She scanned fifteen faces hopefully.

"He's probably sick again," Joey said. "He gets sick a lot."

Lacey's mind raced. If TJ were sick, he might not appear at the performance, either. "Joey, do you think you can sing TJ's part?" Lacey asked.

The little boy's eyes glowed. "We practiced it together lots of times. I know it just as good as he does."

"Just as *well* as he does," Lacey corrected. "Let's try it." And she struck the chord for the third time. This time the children began to sing.

⁊⁊

Letters from home came irregularly. Lacey knew it was difficult to mail a letter from the peninsula and she had not expected that there would be much mail for her. Her family either would have to wait for Gordon Wright to appear and carry a letter, and hope that he would remember to mail it from some town along his route, or they would have to entrust a letter to a lumberjack who might be traveling off the peninsula. Still, she hoped. One note came from Micah, sweetly written in his awkward handwriting. The form was perfect, with a salutation, two paragraphs in the body recounting recent deer sightings in the meadow, and a closing that read, "Sincerely yours, Micah D. Wells." Lacey pictured her mother making a lesson out of writing a letter. No experience was ever wasted if Mary Wells had anything to say about it.

The other letter Lacey received was from Travis. He seemed quite satisfied with work in the lumber camp, too satisfied, in Lacey's opinion. In what little spare time he had, he was helping to build Peter and Abby's new home and was clearly pleased with his new carpentry skills. He asked politely about how her work was going but gave no further indication of his feelings.

Joey's voice glittered in the air as Lacey played the notes on the piano from memory. Joey did, indeed, know the part. His voice was not as unfaltering as TJ's, but he sang earnestly.

The song ended. "Joey, I'm so glad you practiced with TJ," Lacey said enthusiastically. The little boy beamed. "Whatever would we have done if you hadn't learned the part?"

"Are we done now?" Roger wanted to know.

Lacey nodded. "Yes, we're done. I'll see you all at the meeting hall at three o'clock tomorrow afternoon. Don't be late!"

Her students clamored into their coats and bolted through the doorway. Lacey moved to the window to watch them disperse across the clearing and head toward their homes. She could not help wondering where TJ was. He had been a steadfast student throughout the fall semester. He was dedicated and craved learning. But in recent weeks, he had been missing school more and more often. Lacey was not convinced that he was just sick.

eleven

"Miss Wells! Miss Wells!"

Lacey pivoted just in time to find Patsy and Maggie tumbling into her skirts. She stooped to give the six-year-old girls a proper embrace before they knocked her over completely. Patsy slobbered on Lacey's face and that reminded her of Micah.

"Do you like my dress?" Patsy asked, twirling her new calico garb proudly.

"You look very elegant," Lacey replied and Patsy beamed at her teacher with satisfaction.

"When do we sing?" Maggie demanded. "I want to sing!"

Lacey chuckled at her enthusiasm. "Soon, Maggie. It will be our turn soon."

"You said we would sing after lunch. I'm all done eating," Maggie said.

"We have to be patient, Maggie. It won't be much longer."

"When you give the signal, right, Miss Wells?" Patsy asked.

"Right. When I put up our special flag on top of the piano, it will be our turn to sing. Don't forget to watch!"

"We won't," the little girls promised and then scampered off.

Lacey surveyed the crowd. It was a good turnout. Winterfest extended through one entire Saturday. A tradition that had begun in Tyler Creek ten years earlier now beckoned residents from the other small towns in the region. The meeting hall, which served as a church on Sundays, was not built for nearly as many people as were crammed into it that day. But it was the biggest building in Tyler Creek and there was nowhere else to go for the town council refused to take Tyler Creek's

Winterfest to Paxton just for the sake of a bigger space.

The temperature was well below freezing that day and only the most hardened snow fans insisted on outdoor activity. Toboggans sliced their way down the hill, only to be hauled to the top by the next waiting team. An army of snowmen stood guard around the meeting hall, but no one lasted more than a few minutes in the biting wind. With icicles dangling from their clothes, one by one the outdoors enthusiasts sought the refuge and warmth of the meeting hall.

Inside, the temperature climbed steadily throughout the day as more and more people filtered in. The festivities had begun at eight in the morning. Quilts, the products of long winter evenings, adorned the walls of the meeting hall. In one corner men huddled to discuss their optimism for a good spring planting, surely only a few weeks away. Mothers kept one eye on their roaming children and the other on the sketches of new fashions that were making their way around the room. Games for the children lined the far end of the room. At noon, the long tables down one side of the hall were laden with everyone's best potluck dish, providing twice as much food as the hundreds of people there would require. Lacey had eaten heartily, something she had come to regret as her own nerves became unsettled while she considered the fact that the chidren had never before participated in the Winterfest program. Lacey had put herself out on a limb when she had suggested that they should. If the children's performance was not perfect, she would be ridiculed and no one would ever be convinced of the place of music in the educational program at Tyler Creek.

Lacey did not dare leave her music on the piano. Clutching it close so it would not be mangled in an inevitable collision, she scanned the crowd. She looked for one small head that could easily be lost in the throng of milling adults.

Maria came to stand beside her. "Have you spotted him yet?" Maria asked.

Lacey shook her head.

"Perhaps TJ is still ill," Maria offered.

Lacey nodded. "Perhaps. Sally was in school yesterday. When I asked her about her brother, she didn't answer. She acted like she didn't hear me, but I'm certain she did."

"I'm sure it's nothing." Maria abruptly stepped back to let a teenager hurtle past her.

"I'm not so sure," Lacey answered. "I'm worried about TJ. He really wanted to sing that solo. I can't understand why he wouldn't send word to me if he couldn't do it."

Maria shrugged. "Children often change their minds for reasons adults don't understand."

"I had to give his solo away," Lacey said. "I can't take it back from Joey now. But I'm still worried about TJ."

"I'll keep looking," Maria said. "If I find him, I'll tell him you are looking for him." Then Maria faded away as the crowd jostled them.

Lacey was polite to anyone who spoke to her but her mind was on one thing, and at last she glimpsed a swatch of light brown hair that looked familiar. The child stood and watched as other children tossed darts at a target. Smiling at the people she squeezed past, Lacey moved steadily toward the bobbing head. Periodically she lost sight of him, but each time she glimpsed the child, she was more convinced it was TJ. Determined, she made her way past Mrs. Childer's apple pie and the group huddling around Mrs. Graves and her new afghan. She continued past the new calico samples from the mercantile in Paxton and the farmers bartering for horses and cows. Finally, she reached the other end of the hall.

"Hello, TJ!" she called.

The boy barely lifted his eyes. "Hello, Miss Wells."

"I understand you haven't been feeling well." Lacey kept her tone cheerful, while her heart swelled in sympathy.

TJ did not answer. His right foot slid forward and then back again several times. His hands stuffed in his pockets, TJ had not met Lacey's eyes.

"We missed you in school," Lacey said, "especially during

the spelling bee yesterday. I know how much you like the spelling bees."

The foot slid forward again. "Who won?" he asked quietly.

"Roger. He spelled 'educate.' "

TJ nodded. "That's a hard one. But I can spell it."

"I'm sure you can."

TJ turned his head and looked over his shoulder. The black-and-blue patch on the bottom of his chin was unmistakable. When he turned his head again, Lacey saw the mark on his forehead, just under the lock of hair that hung down over his left eye. Fury stirred within her.

"TJ—" she started to say.

His eyes pleaded with her to say no more.

"Are you sure you're all right?" she asked quietly, her tone no longer chipper.

He nodded and looked over his shoulder again.

This time Lacey saw what he had been looking at. Bert Richards approached and he clapped a hand on his son's back. TJ immediately tensed.

"I hope the schoolmarm is not making you do your lessons here," Bert said jovially.

"No, sir," TJ muttered.

"I was just inquiring about TJ's health," Lacey said. "I was concerned that he might not be feeling well yet."

Bert squeezed his son's shoulder in an unconvincing way. "The boy has been sickly lately. But he was just dying to come to Winterfest, and I didn't want to deny him that."

Lacey fumed. *You deny him school*, she thought, *and there's no telling what you do to him at home. But at Winterfest you want us all to believe you have a happy household.*

Aloud, Lacey said, "TJ, when you didn't come to the last practice, I had to give your solo to Joey. But I hope you'll sing with us anyway."

TJ shrugged one shoulder.

"I'm not sure the boy feels well enough for that," Bert said, more loudly than was necessary. "We'll be sure to listen to every note of your little choir, though."

Lacey saw the sneer behind Bert's broad grin. With a flash of horror she realized that TJ had been beaten because of his interest in the choir. She changed the subject.

"Your son is quite a speller, Mr. Richards."

"He's a book learner, that's for sure. Sometimes he forgets to get his nose out of a book to do his chores, ain't that right, son?" Bert clapped TJ's back again.

"Yes, sir."

"Book learning is fine, but a man's got to have his head in the real world."

Lacey could hardly contain herself. "A good education will prepare TJ for a very productive life, no matter what he chooses to do."

"I just don't want him getting airs about himself, that's all." Bert stared deep into Lacey's eyes. "Come on, TJ. I'm sure your teacher has things to take care of."

Bert Richards led his son away. TJ never looked back—because he did not dare, Lacey was sure.

Maria appeared. "I see you found TJ."

Lacey nodded. "Something horrible is going on in that house."

"Lacey, you can't be sure of anything."

Lacey turned and stared at her fellow teacher, whose eyes flickered away. "You know, don't you? And you haven't said a word!"

"It's time for your choir to sing," Maria said. "You'd better get the children together."

Maria turned away. Lacey glanced at the clock. Maria was right. It was time to slither through the crowd back to the piano and give the signal that the children should gather. As soon as the bright orange and blue triangle flag was set on the piano, Patsy and Maggie appeared; Roger, Rebekah, Joey, and the others were not far behind. Many of them had anxiously been waiting nearby for the secret signal.

Lacey's hands shook as she placed her music on the piano

and scooted the bench a few inches closer. The children bumped and jostled until they had finally formed two reasonably straight lines.

"Joey," Lacey said, her voice quavering, "you'd better stand in the front row so everyone can hear you."

"I can't see you, Miss Wells," Patsy complained.

"You may come and stand on this side," Lacey said, "right next to Joey."

More jostling ensued.

Dear Lord, Lacey thought, *still my soul and hands.*

Gradually the notes on the page in front of her fell into a pattern, and Lacey played a lively introduction to get the crowd's attention. Out of the corner of one eye, she saw the thatch of light brown hair. She turned, and at last TJ met her eyes.

twelve

Satisfied that the fire had caught, Lacey leaned against the stove's heavy black door to make sure it shut securely. Then she wrapped her arms around her chest and huddled over the stove, waiting for warmth. Though the morning light had not yet come, she could tell that the early spring day would be a brisk one, and she was determined that her schoolroom would be warm when the children arrived. Four weeks had passed since Winterfest. Spring was stubborn in coming.

When she accepted the teaching contract, it had not occurred to Lacey to ask about things like heating the school. On her second day in Tyler Creek, Maria had meticulously demonstrated how to get the stove started. Then they alternated the chore. In addition to the unpleasantness of leaving her warm bed and going outside while it was still dark, the stubbornness of the stove aggravated Lacey. The door was hinged badly, and she was not convinced that the stove was vented properly.

Gradually she warmed up just in time to dash across the yard to the small house she shared with Maria. She knew Maria would have the fire going and breakfast waiting. A mug of steaming coffee greeted her.

Two hours later, they were both in their classrooms, waiting for the children. Lacey greeted the children at the door, mentally taking attendance as they hung their coats and stored their lunch buckets. The morning bustle was typical; the children chattered with each other and crowded around the stove for warmth. Some of them had walked several miles to come to school. Lacey had learned from experience to allow them a few minutes to recover from the cold outside before insisting that they take their seats.

TJ was missing, again. But Sally was there. Lacey glanced over at the girl's tattered coat on its hook and saw no lunch bucket beneath it. She had not really expected to see one, but she kept hoping.

Then she walked up behind the huddle of children and made herself cheerful. "Good morning, everyone. Are you feeling warmer?"

She glanced at Sally as the children responded, but the girl did not even turn her head to acknowledge the question. Her hair badly needed combing and her dress was much too thin for the weather.

Lacey laid her hand lightly on Sally's shoulder. "Where's TJ? I hope everything's all right."

"He's sick," Sally said sullenly.

"I hope he'll be better soon."

Sally shook her head. "No. He's real sick this time."

Lacey sighed. TJ had been "sick" too often. Sally always gave the same explanation. But Lacey was not fooled for sometimes the bruising and swelling were not quite healed when he returned to school. A lump hardened in her stomach at the thought of what was happening to that eight-year-old boy at the hand of his own father.

"Are we going to do math today?" someone asked and Lacey was pulled back to the task at hand.

"Yes, we're going to work on subtraction. But first, let's finish reading the story we started yesterday."

The children reluctantly left the warmth of the stove and took their seats. The day was underway.

At the lunch break, Lacey was relieved to see some of the other girls offering bits of their lunch to Sally. More than once, she herself claimed to have more food than she could eat and insisted that Sally or TJ help her by eating some bread. But it seemed easier for Sally when the other girls wordlessly set something in front of her. Today she gobbled up a slab of bread with butter and two apples. Obviously she had had no breakfast, and she may not have had anything last night, either. Lacey watched from her desk, trying not to let Sally notice.

After school, Lacey fell in step beside Sally outside the building. "Hi, Sally. I thought I'd walk home with you today. I'd like to check on TJ."

Alarm flashed across the girl's face. "He's sick."

"I know. I'd like to see if there is something I can do to help."

"He'll be sleeping."

Lacey hesitated. "Well, I wouldn't want to disturb him, of course. Perhaps there is something I can do for your mother. I could sit with TJ while she does some of her chores outside."

"I'll do the chores today. No need for you to come."

Lacey could not push the six-year-old girl any farther. The look of fright on her blanched face told the whole story. Something was going on in that house, and Sally did not want her teacher to see it.

"I'll see you tomorrow, Miss Wells." Sally dashed off, running faster than any of the other children and disappearing around the bend in the road.

"What was that all about?" Maria asked.

"I wanted to walk Sally home," Lacey said.

"Why?"

"To see TJ. He was absent again today. Lately, he misses more days than he attends."

"His mother says he's always been a sickly child," Maria observed.

"I don't believe that for a moment, and neither should you!"

"Lacey! What's gotten into you?"

"Open your eyes, Maria. TJ is not sick. Not this time, not any time. His father. . ." She could hardly bring herself to say the words aloud. "His father beats him."

"You don't know that for sure."

"Yes, I do."

"Have you ever seen it happen?"

"No, but—"

"Does he come to school with bruises?"

"He's not allowed to come after it happens, not till the bruises are nearly gone."

Maria shook her head. "Look, Lacey, I'll admit the family is a bit odd. Mrs. Richards will hardly look anyone in the eye, and Sally acts like she's scared to death of something."

"Then you agree!"

Maria held up her hand. "Hold on. I didn't agree to anything. I said the family is unusual. Maybe they have some problems but you have no proof of what you suspect."

"I don't suspect it, I know it!"

"You can't prove it. And you don't want to tangle with Bert Richards."

"Why not?" Lacey asked, defiantly shaking her head.

"Because if you do, you'll stir up this whole community and get a lot of people angry at you. Then what good will you be to anyone?"

"There must be a way!" Lacey insisted.

Maria shook her head. "Do what you can for TJ when he's in school, but stay away from his father, for your own good."

"What about TJ's good?" Lacey snapped.

Maria did not answer. Instead, she pushed a basket she had been holding into Lacey's hands. "Mrs. Larsen came by with a basket of fresh muffins. Would you mind taking them back to the house? I have a meeting with another parent." Lacey was silent but Maria met her eyes before turning around and going back inside the school. She had said all she had to say.

Lacey sighed and looked down at the basket in her arms. She pulled back the napkin for a peek at the muffins. They were still warm and thin steam rose and dissipated in the cool air. Lacey shivered, suddenly feeling the cold, for in her haste to catch Sally, she had not stopped for a coat. The wind whipped her skirt around her ankles and sliced through her. Reluctantly, Lacey retrieved her coat from her classroom, adjusted the stove door, and trudged across the yard to the house, carrying the muffins. Once inside, she sat down on a kitchen chair, cradling the basket in her lap.

She refused to accept that there was nothing more she could do for TJ. Maria was wrong. When she thought of TJ, she could not also help thinking of Micah, with his slender frame and tender disposition. She would never stand for anyone hurting Micah so why should she stand for anyone hurting TJ?

Sally's frightened eyes haunted Lacey. Sally rarely missed school, but she was constantly tired, and so thin!

Lacey looked at the basket of muffins. Many of the children's mothers were generous with gifts for the two teachers, and they always had more than they needed. More than likely, these muffins would go stale before she and Maria could eat them.

Abruptly, Lacey stood up, reached for a box on the bookshelf, and began transferring muffins from the basket to the box. Maria, she knew, would say that Mrs. Larsen would be insulted if she knew they gave away her muffins. But, at the moment, Lacey did not care about that. Sally and TJ needed those muffins more than she did. She tucked one of her own red napkins around the top of the box, turned up the collar on her coat, and headed out the door.

&

The Richards family lived nearly two miles from the school, on the outskirts of the little town. Lacey marched down the road, politely nodding her greetings to passersby but intent on her mission. The Richards house was in need of repair. One window was broken and boards were nailed across it but the wind howled through the cracks. The third step up to the sagging porch had a hole through it and Lacey saw it just in time to step over it.

She knocked on the door and waited. She heard unmistakable scuffling from inside the house, but no one came to the door. She knocked again. "Mrs. Richards? It's Miss Wells. Please open the door."

Lacey saw a tattered curtain move ever so slightly and

caught a glimpse of Sally's profile. She held her breath. After a moment, the door opened about two inches.

"Hello, Mrs. Richards," Lacey said.

"Ain't Sally behavin' herself at school?" Mrs. Richards asked.

"Oh, she's fine. She's doing very good work. I. . .I brought you some muffins," Lacey said, holding the box out. "I know TJ is sick and I thought the muffins might save you some work for supper."

"Thank you, but I already made biscuits."

"Oh. Well, then, perhaps for the morning." Subtly she set them on a half-rotted barrel next to the door. "How is TJ doing?"

"He's mendin'," came the reply, and Lacey noticed the mother's choice of words.

"Might I see him?" Lacey asked.

"He's sleeping now. He needs his rest."

"Of course he does." Lacey looked into the tired eyes of Alvira Richards. She could not have been more than thirty years old, barely ten years older than Lacey herself. But she was worn out and Lacey wondered how much longer she would last.

Despite the knot in her throat, she persisted in her attempt to make conversation. "I hope he'll be able to come back to school tomorrow. We miss him."

"Probably not tomorrow. Maybe the next day."

After the swelling goes down, Lacey thought. Aloud she said, "Please tell him I stopped by."

"No need to leave those muffins," Mrs. Richards said.

"Well, perhaps—"

"You heard what she said!" a voice boomed from behind Lacey.

She wheeled and was face-to-face with Bert Richards. Lacey swallowed hard. "I meant no harm. Just trying to be neighborly."

"You ain't our neighbor. You're the teacher."

"I. . .I. . .I heard TJ was sick. I just wondered how one of my students was doing."

"At school, he's your student. Here he's my boy and he ain't no concern of yours." His voice boomed into her face, and the smell of alcohol sprayed out of his mouth while fire burned in his eyes.

Involuntarily, Lacey took a step backwards. "I meant no harm," Lacey repeated. She glanced at the window and saw Sally, her face scrunched up in horror at what might happen next; Lacey's resolve to confront Bert Richards disintegrated. Obviously, he was raging drunk. There was no telling what might happen to Sally and Alvira if she persisted.

Quickly she turned and went down the steps, intentionally leaving the muffins. She walked as calmly as she could, determined not to run and let Bert think she was afraid of him. From a safe distance, she stepped off the road and slid behind a tree to look back at the house. The porch was deserted, except for the box of muffins topped by the bright red napkin. Her heart pounded.

What am I getting into? she thought. *Lord, You know I mean to help those children. Show me how.*

thirteen

Lacey sniffed her dripping nose, wiped a tear with the back of her hand, and reached for a fresh sheet of paper. A half-dozen crumpled sheets were scattered across the small table next to the stove in the cottage. She had been trying for an hour to find the right words for the letter. Dipping her pen into the inkwell once again, she made another attempt.

> *Dear Members of the Board,*
> *It is with great regret that I tender my resignation as teacher of the lower elementary grades at the Tyler Creek School, effective immediately. I am not unmindful of the inconvenience this will cause. Nevertheless, I believe my action to be in the best interest of the children.*

That she must resign, Lacey was sure. After her encounter with Bert Richards, she had stumbled back to the cottage, shaken and befuddled about what to do next. Somewhere, about halfway home, her confusion got the best of her. If she could not reach out to a child like TJ, and actually help him, then she had no business calling herself a teacher and all the children would be better off with someone more competent, both in the classroom and with the families of the students.

Sighing, Lacey laid down her pen. If she left Tyler Creek, she would have to go home to the peninsula. Where else could she go? After her grandmother in Milwaukee had died, the rest of her mother's family had moved west. Papa's siblings were scattered around the country, too, and none of them would welcome a wayward niece who had failed at the first job she ever had. What other skills did she have except teaching? No, she had nowhere to go except home. From Tyler Creek she could take the train as far as she could and then follow the land route in the back of a jarring wagon. She would go home a failure, and her mother would be proven right that Lacey was not ready to leave the peninsula.

Lacey snatched up her paper and crumpled it into the seventh wad. How could she even think of going home? No explanation in the world would be good enough to offer to Travis. He had gone to a great deal of trouble to get her this job. She did not want to face the disappointment she would see in his eyes if she left Tyler Creek now.

On the other hand, how long would she be home before Travis noticed? She had barely heard from him in seven months, and even then he kept his feelings carefully hidden. His few letters summarized life in the lumber camp with interesting language but far more detail than Lacey wished for and closed with a bit of news about her family. He said little about himself or his own plans. He had already stayed at the camp a full year, far longer than he originally intended.

What did I expect? Lacey asked herself. *Did I think that if I did what he wanted me to do and took this job, he would give me undying admiration? Why did he think I could do this? He's thrown me to the wolves.*

Lacey wiped her nose and chided herself for thinking such harsh thoughts about Travis. He had not forced her to come to Tyler Creek. When she signed the contract with the school board, she was truly excited about the challenge that lay before her. But she had not counted on Bert Richards. She was almost at the end of her contract with only two months remaining. Lacey put the lid on her box of paper. She had made a promise and she would fulfill it.

The door creaked open, and Maria entered. "What is all this?" she asked, pointing at the seven wads of paper.

"I tried to write my letter of resignation," Lacey confessed.

"Why would you do that?" Maria hung her coat on the peg beside the door.

"Because I'm no good here, that's why."

"From what I have observed, you have the makings of a fine teacher. You just need some experience in the classroom."

Lacey rose to her feet and grabbed at the wads of paper. "Is experience in the classroom going to tell me what to do with Bert Richards?"

"Don't tell me you went out to the Richards' place."

"All right, I won't tell you."

"But you did."

Lacey nodded.

Maria sighed heavily. "I know you mean well, Lacey. You would move heaven and earth for that boy. But what you did today did not help him."

"I know that," Lacey mumbled as she opened the stove door and dropped her wads into the coals. She watched them catch and burst brilliantly before sizzing into cinders. "But I couldn't just do nothing."

Maria took a pot off a hook and filled it with water. "I'll fix you something to eat. Where are the muffins I sent home with you?"

"I took them to the Richards."

"Then we'll have no bread for supper."

"We could never have eaten all those muffins before they went stale."

"We could have eaten two with our supper while they were fresh." Maria whacked at a carrot and tossed the pieces into the pot.

"Sorry," Lacey mumbled.

"It's no matter. We have a bit of dried beef from the Muellers and plenty of potatoes. I'll have a pot of soup ready before you know it."

"I'm not really hungry."

"Apparently not, or you would not have given away our muffins."

Lacey sank into the easy chair. "Maria, how do you do it?"

"I've been making soup since I was ten." Maria thwacked a potato.

"You know what I mean," Lacey prodded. "You've been teaching here for years. Bert Richards can't be the first difficult parent you've ever known."

"Some children don't get to come to school at all," Maria said, "especially girls. I take the ones I can get and try to open their minds to learning, so that no matter where they end up they will want to learn."

"And the ones you can't get?"

"I can't save the world, Lacey Wells, and neither can you." Maria set the pot on the stove and stirred the contents.

"Is that what you think I'm doing?"

"I imagine that's what Bert Richards thinks you're trying to do. And that's not going to help TJ."

"I've made a mess of everything. Maybe I should work on that resignation letter again."

"And what good will that do?" Maria had a point.

"Maria," Lacey said, "I know you are not very religious but do you believe in having a calling? Are you here because you have a calling for teaching?"

"I'm here because there's a job to be done," Maria said simply as she took two bowls down from a shelf.

"But how do you know if this is the job you should be doing?"

"I'm here, aren't I?"

"You could be teaching in Milwaukee or Detroit or anywhere else," Lacey challenged. "Why are you in Tyler Creek?"

"I'm far too practical for these philosophical questions," Maria responded. "There is a great deal of work to be done right here in Tyler Creek, and I've invested seven years already. I don't need to look any further."

Maria Johnson and Daniel Wells had a lot in common, Lacey decided. There was a job to be done and they were in the right place to do it.

Sinking back in the easy chair, Lacey watched Maria work. As the soup simmered, Maria stacked the dishes from earlier in the day and wiped off the butcher block where she had chopped the vegetables. Lacey made a mental note to offer to do the dishes after supper. She tried to do her share of the housework, but in many ways the cottage was Maria's home in a way that it would never be Lacey's. The dishes were stacked the way Maria liked them and the furniture placed the way with which Maria was comfortable. Maria moved around the small kitchen competently and efficiently. She was home here; she belonged.

But do I belong? Lacey asked herself. *Will I ever belong anywhere?*

"Come and eat," Maria said, ladling the soup into the bowls.

"I'm sorry about the muffins." Lacey said, as she pulled herself out of the overstuffed chair and moved to the table.

"Pay no mind. It's just as well we have no muffins. I'm getting far too plump."

"You have a practical perspective on everything."

"That's how the work gets done."

Lacey sat and put a napkin in her lap. She paused to give silent thanks for the meal, knowing that Maria was watching her out of politeness. Lifting a spoon, Lacey said, "You remind me of both of my parents at the same time, if that's possible."

"Anything is possible," Maria responded.

Lacey chuckled. "And that sounds like a friend of mine."

"The friend who suggested you for this position?"

Lacey nodded. "But maybe being practical is not always the right thing to do."

"It has always worked for me."

"Maybe so, but I'm not sure it will work for TJ Richards."

Maria looked at her, puzzled. "We've come a far piece from talking about your resignation, haven't we?"

Lacey tasted the soup. "Yes, I suppose we have."

"Well, you can just put any thought of resigning out of your head once and for all. It's the most impractical thing I've heard in weeks."

"Why?"

"You signed a contract. You can't just walk away from that. Where will the board find a teacher to fill in? And what about the children who have grown fond of you already? Will TJ be better off if you leave now? You only have a few weeks left. There's a job to be done. Stay and do it."

Lacey sighed. "I suppose you're right. Staying is the sensible thing to do."

"Stay, and enjoy it!" Maria admonished.

That Lacey could not promise. If she had to spend the next two months watching TJ suffer, how could she enjoy Tyler Creek?

fourteen

As Lacey walked, she fingered the letters in the pocket of her skirt. Micah's letter, flawlessly spelled and punctuated with the lettering in perfect, straight lines, reported that he had at last been allowed to help polish the brass railing around the top of the lighthouse. "Papa is persuaded I shall not be careless and tumble from the balcony," Micah had written. "I got brass polish under all my fingernails." In her mind, Lacey could see the pride beaming from her little brother's face.

The letter from Travis was the fourth he had sent since Lacey had arrived in Tyler Creek. The first three were enthusiastic reports of the booming lumber business on the peninsula. Travis had begun to speak of the lumber camp as if it were a small town. But it was the fourth letter that Lacey now carried in her pocket and her heart. At long last, Travis had written how much he missed her and how much he was looking forward to her homecoming in another six weeks.

Six weeks! Since her disastrous—in her eyes—encounter with Bert Richards, Lacey had thought of little else but how to finish out her contract with dignity. Long after Maria finished marking papers and went to bed, Lacey sat up with her books spread around the small table. All her carefully constructed lessons were stacked neatly in a box. Even if I never use these again, she told herself, I will do the very best job I can as long as I am in Tyler Creek. Then she could go home holding her head high, having done her job well.

Still, six weeks seemed an interminable time to wait for release and, despite her long hours with the candle, Lacey was not convinced that things were getting better in the classroom. The two older boys still sat in the back and whispered, although not as often. The younger children seemed genuinely fond of their teacher, and she of them, but she was not sure what would happen when examination time came. Lately, TJ had been in school more than usual, and for this Lacey was grateful. Perhaps her appearance at the Richards house had done some good after all. Drunk as he was, Bert Richards might have realized that he would eventually face the consequences of his actions. Lacey liked to think her trip had not been wasted, but still she heeded Maria's advice and stayed away from the Richards home.

At every opportunity, though, she paid special attention to TJ. But he was painfully thin and seemed distracted most of the time. Lacey shared her lunches and encouraged his every effort but she could not make him stop staring out the window, sullen and silent.

One Sunday afternoon, after having attended church in the meeting hall, Lacey had pushed her papers aside, put on her sturdiest shoes, and had headed for the fields beyond Tyler Creek. The day was brisk and bright, with billowing clouds riding the breeze, and Lacey imagined that Micah would be lying on his back in the meadow behind the house, calling out the animals he saw riding the clouds. She wondered if TJ ever did that.

Despite the logic of her mind, her feet carried her down the dirt road toward the Richards' farm. She had promised Maria she would not go there again for her presence at the Richards place would pose too much of a danger to TJ, and maybe even to Sally. Even so, her feet seemed to follow that path for there was a pleasant clearing that reminded her of the clearing on the peninsula, the place where she had met Travis on Sunday afternoons last spring and summer. With Travis's letter in her pocket, she wanted to be in that clearing.

She reached her destination and stopped for a drink from her water jug. With her back to a tree, she faced northwest, in the direction of home. Lacey took the letter from her skirt pocket and unfolded it once again. She settled into a comfortable position on the ground to read it.

> Dear Lacey,
>   Ed is heading down to Milwaukee for a few weeks with his family. I did not want to miss the opportunity to mail a letter. As wonderful as the peninsula is, I do miss regular mail service!
>   In a few weeks, you will be home and we will have the whole summer together. I hope you will want to meet me in the clearing on Sunday afternoons. I've missed you quite profoundly in the months you've been gone, and I am eager to be together once again, at least until the fall. I imagine you will seek another teaching position, so I must take full advantage of every moment we have together during the summer.
>
> Fondly,
> Travis

ba.

The breeze stirred and the clouds morphed into new configurations. "Lord, You make such beautiful things," Lacey prayed aloud. "Why is Travis's heart not as clear to me as this day? And what do You really want me to do for TJ? I'm listening. Help me to hear Your voice above the others."

A sneeze made Lacey start and she scrambled to her knees and looked around. Another sneeze came and she asked, "Who's there?"

"It's me," a voice answered.

But, as timid as the voice was, Lacey recognized it. "TJ, where are you?"

The bushes behind her parted and TJ crawled out. Instinctively, Lacey scanned his face and arms for new marks. His forearms were bright red. "Are you all right?" she asked.

He nodded. "Who were you talking to?"

Lacey responded with a puzzled look. "No one. I'm alone,

just out for a walk on a fine day."

"But I heard you say something."

"Oh, I was praying. I didn't realize I had spoken aloud."

"Praying?"

"Talking to God about some of the things I'm concerned about."

"Who's Travis?"

"A friend," Lacey said firmly. She could not ignore the fresh marks any longer. "Are you sure you're all right?"

He nodded again and stuffed his hands into the pockets of his overalls. "It's not as bad as usual. My mama told me to get out and stay away for a few hours. By the time I get back, he'll be sleeping it off."

"Oh, TJ, I'm so sorry."

"It's okay. I should be able to come to school tomorrow."

"Of course I'm glad you're not hurt more seriously, but he shouldn't be doing this to you."

"He don't mean no harm. He just gets mad about stupid things when he drinks."

"But he seems to be drinking all the time now."

TJ sat down next to Lacey. "You were praying about me, weren't you?"

"Yes, I was. I believe God wants me to help you, but I'm just not sure how."

"Ain't nothin' you can do. Excuse me, there *isn't* nothin' you can do."

"You mean 'There isn't anything you can do,' " Lacey said, finishing the correction that TJ had begun. "But I can't accept that."

TJ shrugged. "Other folks do. They say you have trouble mindin' your own business."

"Yes, I know they say that."

"Seems true, don't it?"

"Doesn't it. No, I don't think so. I just have a different idea of what's my business than other people do."

"Am I your business?" TJ asked, looking up at Lacey.

"I think you are," Lacey said softly.

"Did God send you to me?"

"I think maybe He did."

"Am I God's business, too?"

Lacey's heart filled her chest. "Of course, you are."

"Then why did He wait so long to send you?"

The question cut through Lacey. How could she possibly think about abandoning TJ?

"TJ," she said, "how would you like it if you didn't go home?"

"You mean today?"

"Yes, for today, maybe a few days."

"Maybe not ever?" he asked.

Lacey nodded. "Maybe until your father gets better."

"Where would I go?"

"Well, to begin with, you could come home with me."

"Miss Johnson won't like that."

"No, I don't suppose she will. But you let me worry about Miss Johnson. You concentrate on keeping yourself safe."

"Would I have a bed?"

"Of course."

"And lunch? Would I get to eat lunch?"

"I promise you will eat lunch every day."

TJ turned his head in the direction of his home. "You make it sound right nice."

"It would be nice. And your father wouldn't hurt you."

"Yes, he would. Somebody would make me go back to my own folks, and he would be steaming mad that I left."

Lacey picked up one of TJ's bony hands. "TJ, I can't make any promises about what will happen next. But if you want to come home with me, I will do my best to protect you and make sure no one hurts you."

TJ slowly shook his head from side to side as a tear rolled down one cheek. "I can't go with you."

"Yes, you can," Lacey urged.

"No, I can't. If I leave, he'll start in on Sally. As long as

I'm there, he leaves her alone."

Lacey squeezed his hand.

"No, I can't go. Sally is too little. She can't run as fast as I can. I have to protect her."

"What if we found a safe place for Sally, too?"

Still, TJ shook his head. "That would break Mama's heart. Sally is her special baby. She would die if Sally went away, she would just die."

Lacey held back her own tears. She tried to imagine Micah, at the tender age of eight, taking on the responsibility for the safety and welfare of two other people. Rage swelled within her at the thought of Alvira Richards allowing, her small son to be in such a position. But Alvira would never leave her husband, of that Lacey was sure.

"I'd better be goin'." TJ stood up abruptly and wiped the tear from his cheek.

"But you can't go home!" Lacey insisted.

"Not yet. I'll wait a while."

"I'll stay with you."

TJ shook his head emphatically. "No, you'd best be on your way, too."

Lacey stood, also. "If you change your mind, TJ—"

"I won't. But if you really think I'm God's business, you might ask if He has another idea."

Lacey could not help but smile. "I will, TJ, I will."

TJ turned, plunged his hands into his pockets once again, and shuffled away from her. He did not look back.

He was small and thin. Lacey had learned a lot from having four younger brothers. She wanted to run after him. She knew she could swoop him up and carry him off, and he would not be strong enough to stop her. Instead, she leaned against the tree and prayed, *Lord, be with him. Let him know that he is Your business.*

fifteen

Lacey cast a sharp look at Denys and Dalton, the older boys in the back of the classroom. Those two were more exasperating than Joel and Jeremiah on their worst days. Three times during the semester Lacey had separated them and then relented and let them sit together. It did not seem fair to seat them with younger children, whom they would only torment endlessly. If they were together, at least they kept their scuffling among themselves. But why was it so difficult for them to understand that silent reading time meant no talking?

Pretending that they had not seen Lacey's look, the boys shuffled apart and turned to their books. Lacey's eyes wandered around the classroom. Even with her own books, brought from the peninsula, there were not enough to go around at reading time. Some of the younger children shared simple storybooks. Patsy, Maggie, and Rebekah, always eager to please the teacher, had read everything in their grade level at least four times. Soon, Lacey would let them attempt some of the longer books.

TJ clutched his book with both hands and buried his face in it. If he heard the whispering behind him or the chairs scraping in front of him, he did not let on. Only the words on the page mattered; his lips moved as he struggled to make out the sounds.

Lacey watched him. He had missed far too much school this semester, and probably every semester since he first started school. He was a bright boy, but too many missed lessons and too little food and sleep made it difficult for him to keep up. Lacey hated to think that in a couple of years TJ would be one of the bigger boys at the back of the classroom, that is if he stayed in school at all.

Lacey turned back to her own book. When the children read,

she read also. It was the pattern she had learned from her own mother more than fifteen years ago. Reading was important, and if it was important for children to do, it was important enough that children should see adults doing it. So she read.

She straightened her chair and turned a page at the same time, and the two sounds covered the noise of the classroom door opening. Lacey's brown-haired head remained bent over her novel. It was only a few minutes before the whispers swelled into murmurs, and she had to lift her head to see the reason. She stifled a gasp and rose to her feet. What was Travis Gates doing, standing in the back of her classroom?

Grabbing for composure, she smiled at the children and walked down the aisle between the desks to meet him in the back. As she passed each row, curious heads turned to follow her path.

"What a surprise!" she whispered. She wanted to embrace him, but she dared not in front of the children. "What are you doing here?"

"Visiting you, of course."

"But it's so far from the peninsula. Are you on your way home to the city? Have you left the lumber camp?"

He smiled and shook his head. "No, I love it there. But I got wind that a friend of mine was coming this way, and I couldn't pass up the chance to see you."

"And Tom Saget let you go?"

"I didn't give him a choice."

Lacey's heart warmed in a way it had not for weeks. "How long can you stay?"

"Just for the evening. I leave on the early morning train out of Paxton."

"Oh."

"Sorry it couldn't be longer."

"You've come a long way for an evening."

"I'm sure I won't regret it."

Travis's eyes held Lacey motionless. What did it mean that he had gone to such lengths to see her?

"Miss Wells," Patsy said as she tugged on her teacher's sleeve, "who is that man?"

Lacey jumped back to reality. The entire class had twisted in their chairs to watch her conversation. The older boys snickered; the little girls glowed with curiosity. She pushed out a quick breath and said, "We'd better get this over with."

"Class," Lacey said in a loud, steady voice, "this is Mr. Gates, a friend of mine. I hope you will give him a warm welcome to Tyler Creek." Then, leaving Travis behind, Lacey marched with a straight back to the front of the room. "We are just about out of time today. In the morning, we will begin with arithmetic."

The groans were louder than the cheers as the children pushed back their wooden benches, gathered their lunch buckets, and prepared to leave.

"I like arithmetic," said Patsy.

Lacey smiled and stroked the child's head. "I know you do. And you're wonderful at doing sums."

"Are we going to have spelling tomorrow?" asked Maggie.

"In the afternoon," Lacey assured her.

Travis leaned against the back wall and watched with contentment as Lacey moved around the classroom helping her students collect their things. It seemed to him that she was quite comfortable and confident in the role. Her letters had described the room well, including the two boys in the back who were likely to drop out soon. But she had underestimated her ability to handle herself in the classroom. She had described nervousness and anxiety, but he saw only warmth and competence. She showed the same tenderness toward her students that he had seen her give to Micah.

What her letters had not said, however, was how she felt about being off the peninsula, and whether she would ever want to return to live there. He hoped so, because he wanted her to return. But it would have to be her choice.

TJ was taking longer than the others to gather his things, so Lacey crossed to his desk and asked, "Are you all right?"

TJ smiled slyly. "This is the friend you were praying

about, isn't it?"

Lacey felt the blush rise in her cheeks. "Yes, this is my friend."

"Did God answer your questions yet?"

"Not entirely. I'm still listening."

"When He tells you about His business, let me know, okay?"

"Of course. Now why don't you catch up with Sally and walk home together?" TJ scuffled out of the building and Lacey was left alone with Travis.

"What was that all about?" Travis asked, smiling, and Lacey wondered just how much Travis had heard.

"Just following up a conversation we had on the side of the road one day," she said. Then, restraining herself no further, she opened her arms to Travis, who took her in tightly. She buried her face in his chest and breathed in his scent. "It's so good to see you," she said.

"I was hoping you would say something like that," came his gentle reply.

"I've been so homesick," Lacey admitted.

"You? Homesick?" Travis stroked the back of Lacey's head. "I didn't think you would admit to missing the peninsula."

Lacey laughed. "Don't tattle on me to my mother." She picked up her shawl and led the way out of the classroom and down the path that led out of Tyler Creek.

"Micah misses you terribly," Travis said. "He wants to write you a letter every day, but of course your mother is too sensible for that."

"Of course."

"She makes him stick to his lessons, and reminds him that he can mail a letter only when Gordon Wright comes anyway."

"And the twins? They haven't written a single word."

"Rambunctious as ever, but your mother does her best to keep them reined in. I was there for their twelfth birthday party."

"I've never missed a birthday before. Now I've missed all my brothers' birthdays."

"Micah is quite proud of being eight, instead of a mere seven."

"I'm sure he is."

"Joshua tries to go home every Sunday now."

"I'm sure that makes Mama happy. How is my father?"

Travis shrugged. "You know your father. He doesn't say much, but I know he wonders how you're doing."

"He hasn't written. But putting words on paper would be hard for him."

Travis looked back over his shoulder. The row of buildings had disappeared behind them. "Are we out of town already?"

Lacey laughed. "It's not much of an effort to get out of Tyler Creek. There's almost as much wide open space around here as there is on the peninsula."

"Are you disappointed that it's not a bigger place?" he asked.

Lacey grinned. "I still think I could do well living in a real city, but Tyler Creek has its own charms, as well as its own troubles." She gestured widely ahead of them. "Off in this direction are several farms. Some of the children come in to go to school, but many of them don't stay past the fourth grade."

"How is school going?"

Lacey rolled her eyes. "I'm doing the very best job I can. I'm just not sure it's enough."

"What do you mean?" Travis responded. "I saw you with the little girl who tugged on your arm and with the boy who left last. They both seemed quite fond of you."

"Yes, I suppose they are."

"Then what's the problem?"

"The people here live difficult lives. Some of them are trapped in vicious circles that go on for generations." Somehow she could not bring herself to speak of TJ in detail.

"Then what you are doing is important. Education can be the way out for some of these children—better jobs, stronger families."

"I want to believe that," Lacey said softly, "but I don't know if book learning can touch the problems they have. I have to keep reminding myself that God can."

"I had no idea Tyler Creek was such a dismal place. I should have never suggested you come here."

Lacey put her hand on Travis's arm. "Oh, no! You did the right thing. And it's not dismal all the time. Some of the families here are doing quite well. We had a wonderful community festival a few weeks ago. The children sang, and they did beautifully."

"So you're not sorry you came?" he asked.

Lacey shook her head. "Every day I want to go home. And every day I'm glad I came."

Travis tilted his head back and laughed. "I suppose in an odd way, that makes sense."

"Tell me about Abby," Lacey pleaded.

"Hasn't she written?"

"Not one word."

"I suppose she hasn't felt well enough to write."

"Abby's ill?" Lacey asked, alarmed.

Travis smiled. "Not ill, exactly. Expecting."

"Expecting?"

"Yes. A little one. A baby."

Lacey's eyes grew wide. "Abby and Peter are having a baby?"

"Yes, it's to be born in the late summer."

"I suppose it was only logical that they would want to have a family. I just didn't think it would happen so fast."

"Their house will be finished soon," Travis said excitedly. "It's not large, but it is quite grand. Peter has been meticulous about every detail. I've learned a lot of carpentry skills working with him."

"So they are really going to settle in and raise a family in the lumber camp."

"It won't be just a camp for long," Travis said. "You'll see. It's becoming more like a town every day.

Lacey shook her head in shock. Inwardly she wondered, *Could I be happy doing what Abby's doing? As inadequate as I feel in Tyler Creek, would I be happier married and living in a lumber camp?*

"We'd better turn back," Lacey said aloud. "Maria will want to meet you."

sixteen

"I have to warn you," Lacey said to Travis as they approached the cottage, "Maria is rather direct."

"That can be an admirable quality," Travis responded. "Does she know who I am?"

"She only knows that a friend helped me find this job." Lacey pushed open the door and they stepped into the cozy kitchen. Maria was bent over a steaming pot. She looked up.

"So this is your friend, Mr. Gates?" Maria asked.

Lacey and Travis exchanged a look. Smiling, Travis extended his hand to Maria. "Travis Gates, at your service. It is a pleasure to meet you."

"Travis, this is Maria Johnson," Lacey said to complete the introduction. She glanced at the table, set for three. "How did you know—"

"That your friend would stay for supper? Where else would he eat? Tyler Creek doesn't have a restaurant, unless you count Selma Parker's annual summer picnic buffet."

"But how did you know he was here?"

Maria chuckled. "Everyone in Tyler Creek knows. Mr. Gates here hitched a ride in with Tom Saunders, who wastes no time remarking on strangers. And of course the children in your classroom were quite fascinated that someone would appear so unexpectedly."

"There was no time to write," Travis explained. "It was a spur of the moment trip."

"Of course," Maria said as she stirred her pot.

"I would have cooked. After all, Travis is my guest," Lacey said.

"No need for fussing. Everything's under control. You two enjoy yourselves."

Lacey felt the blush rise in her cheeks. "Then, what can I do to help you?"

"Not a thing," Maria said. "The two of you should make yourselves comfortable in the sitting room. With a little notice, I might have prepared a meal worthy of our guest, but I'm afraid we'll have to settle for boiled chicken. We don't want to waste any time. Tom Saunders will be looking for Mr. Gates before long."

"Tom is taking you back into Paxton?" Lacey asked.

"He kindly offered," Travis said, "and I was afraid you wouldn't have a carriage."

"We've got a wagon and an old mare," Maria said, "but Lacey would have no business driving into Paxton by herself late at night. Shoo. Go sit down. I'll call you when the food is ready."

Obediently, Lacey and Travis moved to the other room, hardly out of earshot of the kitchen.

"Is she always like this?" Travis asked, his voice hardly above a whisper.

Lacey covered her mouth to conceal her laugh. "Not this bad, usually. But we don't get many guests."

"We'd better keep talking," Travis said softly.

Lacey took his cue. "How was the train ride?" she asked in a louder voice.

"A bit bumpy."

"I suppose the tracks need some repairs."

"Yes, I suppose so."

Maria poked her head around the corner. "You two will have to do better than that. I would think you would have more to discuss than the quality of Wisconsin's railroad ties. Come to the table for some real conversation."

Holding back their laughter, Lacey and Travis obediently moved to the table. Maria gestured that they should sit next to each other, and she settled into a chair across from them. Lacey gave thanks for the food then raised the platter for Travis to serve himself.

"I hope Lacey has been telling you all the delightful things she has been doing," Maria said.

Travis's eyes lit up. "I'd like to hear about that."

"Then she hasn't told you?"

"I was anxious to hear news from home," Lacey said in her own defense.

"Of course, but your family will also want news of you when Travis returns."

"Tell me all the wonderful things she has been doing," Travis urged.

"The first thing that comes to mind is the choir for Winterfest," Maria started. "We've got that wretched piano in the back of the schoolhouse, but until now no one bothered to see what it could do. Lacey worked wonders with the children, despite the fact that the piano hasn't been tuned in twenty years."

"Why didn't you write me about that?" Travis chided.

"It was just a couple of songs," Lacey said. "Simple ones I learned from my mother. All my brothers would be able to sing them."

"But the children here don't get music like that," Maria said. "You brought that to them. I'm sure they'll want to do it again next year."

Travis's head snapped toward Lacey. "Next year? Will you still be here?"

She shook her head. "No, my contract runs out in June. I'm sure of that."

"Someone else will have to take it up, then," Maria said. "Everyone enjoyed the performance. Some of the students who have a difficult time in the classroom sang quite nicely. It was good to see them succeed at something."

Lacey scooped some rice onto her plate. "But I'm not sure I'm reaching those children with their lessons."

"Of course, you are. From everything I've seen, Dalton and Denys are at last ready to move up into my classroom. They'll have a much better attitude about school once they are in with the older children. You haven't let them dawdle for a single day."

Travis smiled. "That sounds exactly like the teacher you had, Lacey."

Mary Wells did not believe in dawdling, that much was certain. Lacey had learned well from watching her mother handle Joel and Jeremiah together.

"Ask her about the reading chart," Maria urged.

Travis complied. "What about the reading chart?"

"It's nothing, really," Lacey said, "just a chart that shows all the books the children have read this semester."

"And is it a lot?"

"There aren't many books."

"Nonsense," Maria interjected. "Nobody has been able to get those children to read as much as you have. I can't wait until they're all old enough for my class."

"Lacey didn't say a word about any of this," Travis said. He looked at Lacey with a pride she had not seen in his eyes before. Hastily, she looked away and concentrated on her green beans.

"And I suppose she didn't say anything about the class play, either?" Maria said.

"No, not a word."

"The children have written their own play, to be performed on the last day of the school year," Lacey supplied.

"That's quite an undertaking."

"The credit belongs to my mother," Lacey explained. "She used to make Joshua and me write plays when she was schooling us."

"When I go back to the peninsula, I'll be sure to let her know that her legacy has extended to Tyler Creek."

"All the parents are quite pleased with Lacey," Maria said. "Many of them have told me so. Of course, there are always one or two who simply cannot be pleased, and their children do not get everything from school that they might. But Lacey is a fiesty one," Maria continued. "I suppose growing up on that remote peninsula has made her quite independent."

"Yes, I suppose so," Travis said thoughtfully.

"Perhaps she's too fiesty and independent," Maria continued. "When she gets an idea in her head, she means to do it, even if it means tangling with a man like Bert Richards."

"Who is Bert Richards? And why shouldn't Lacey tangle with him?" Travis's questions bore an edge of concern.

Lacey quickly explained. "I promised I wouldn't go back, not beause I was worried about myself, but because I was concerned for the rest of the family."

"I'm just glad you came to your senses," Maria said sternly.

"TJ hasn't been 'sick' since I went," Lacey observed.

"I do hope you'll be careful," Travis said.

Lacey grabbed a plate of biscuits and thrust them at Travis. "This is a delicious supper, Maria," she said. "You must let me cook for the next few nights."

"Selma Parker is sending Sam over with a ham tomorrow," Maria said. "That should keep us going for a while."

Travis ate a biscuit eagerly. "For some reason we don't get food like this in the mess hall at the lumber camp. I wish I could send the cook over for a few lessons."

"I'll send some biscuits back with you," Maria offered.

"Thank you. I would like that. Has Lacey mentioned her friend Abby to you? She married one of the lumberjacks. She takes pity on me and invites me for supper nearly every Thursday night."

"Abby was never any good at cooking!" Lacey said.

"She is now. You'd be surprised what you can learn to do when you have to."

"Oh, I don't know," Lacey said lightly. "I've learned to keep that decrepit stove in the classroom going. If I had a pitchfork, I'm sure I could tune the piano."

"I don't doubt that you could do anything you sent your mind to do," Travis said.

"She's proven that already," Maria added.

Travis pushed his chair back. "I hope you'll let me help you clean up."

"Certainly not." Maria snatched his plate from him and stacked it on top of her own. "Tom will be here soon. Lacey can walk you out to the road."

Lacey shrugged. They both knew there was no point in arguing with Maria. Lacy wrapped her wool shawl around her shoulders and led the way.

"Maria recited quite a litany of your accomplishments," Travis said.

"When I came, I was full of ideas, most of them from my mother, actually. I have a whole new perspective on what she did for us."

"She would be proud to know what you are doing for these children."

"I'm doing what I can. But I'll be gone in a few weeks. Victoria will be back in the fall. All I've really done is keep things going in her absence."

"I think you've done far more than that."

"Will it matter in the end?" Lacey asked. "After I leave Tyler Creek, I'll never see these children again. How will I know if anything I did helped TJ Richards have a better life?"

"Do you remember how we used to climb the stairs to the tower?" Travis asked.

Lacey nodded, confused.

"I didn't know the way in the darkness. But you did. I had to trust you for every step we took. You know what I'm saying, don't you?"

Lacey nodded again. "Yes, I think so."

"We have to go a step at a time. Someone else is carrying the light and knows where He's leading you."

They reached the edge of the road and turned toward each other. "I'm proud of you, Lacey. You should be proud of yourself," Travis said.

She turned her face up and searched his eyes. Was pride

all that he felt? "I'm glad you came," she said, "even for a few hours."

"So am I."

A few yards away, a carriage rattled toward them.

"There's Tom," Lacey said.

Quickly, smoothly, Travis bent his head and kissed her mouth. Lacey smiled in the darkness.

The carriage rumbled to a stop. "Evenin', ma'am," Tom Saunders said.

"Good evening, Tom. How are you?"

"I'm right fine. I'll make sure your friend here gets to town safely." And Travis was gone into the darkness.

Leaning against the fence, Lacey turned and faced the cottage. The old kerosene lamp glowed in the kitchen where Maria worked.

I should go in and help her, Lacey told herself.

But Lacey wanted to savor the evening for just a moment more. Travis had come to her.

seventeen

The weeks since Travis's visit whirled around Lacey so fast she could barely keep up. Maria had hinted that Lacey should plant the year's vegetable garden, since she had been consuming last year's harvest of green beans, turnips, and carrots for the last few months. It seemed only fair, so Lacey did not protest. She had helped her mother plant a vegetable garden since the time she was two and even the thought of putting in a garden made Lacey hear the hymns her mother used to hum while she worked.

Every afternoon, in the oldest muslin dress she had brought with her, Lacey crouched in the dirt and plunged her fingers into the silky black soil. The birds were far too interested in what she was doing, and before long she had taken on the task of rigging a crude scarecrow.

"That's not a very menacing face," Maria commented one day.

"But he's good and big," Lacey responded. "That's what frightens the birds."

"Victoria has never been much help with the garden for she is too much of a city girl. But you seem to know what you're doing."

Lacey smiled as she surveyed her tidy rows, marked off with string and miniature signs to tell Maria what she had planted and where. Lacey had planted more variety than practical Maria would have bothered with: tomatoes, green beans, radishes, corn, sugar snap peas, and lettuce. Mary Wells would have been proud of the sight.

"You and Victoria will be well-fed next year," she said to Maria.

Maria scowled. "I don't think Victoria will come back."

Lacey snapped her head around. "Not be back? Why not?"
"It's just a feeling I have."

≈

As the garden sprouted, rehearsals for the end-of-the-year class play intensified, and every afternoon was taken up with working on the play. What had begun as a short skit billowed into a full-scale theatrical production. The older children in the class had written a script that Lacey thought was quite clever, although she had had to expand it to create enough parts for everyone in the class. For weeks, the students had been pilfering hats and odd clothing from their parents' closets and arriving at school with pieces of small furniture in tow. The youngest girls had cut and pasted elaborate invitations for all the children to take home.

Only two days remained now and Lacey was unsure of what to expect. She hoped that enough of the parents would come to the performance so that the class would not be entirely disappointed.

But, even without the pending performance, the children would have been agitated, Lacey was certain. An ambivalent spring had burst into robust summer, and Lacey found herself frequently reorganizing and enlivening her lessons to keep the children focused on their assignments. If she left them to do silent reading or sums for very long, their heads would turn and stare out the open window. At the lunch break they tumbled out of the building to frolic in the grass, and they resisted as long as they dared the bell that beckoned them back.

In two days, the performance would be over, and so would the school year. In three days, Lacey would be on a train heading north to the peninsula. There she would spend the summer and sort out her feelings about teaching. Maria insisted that Lacey was doing a spectacular job and had no hesitations to say so to anyone who would listen. But Lacey had such a difficult time separating classroom instruction from the rest of her students' lives. What would it matter if she taught a six year old to do sums if no one else cared that the child could do them?

TJ's attendance during the spring had been better than the winter months. Sometimes his father kept him home to do chores, but Sally no longer reported that he was "sick." A knot tightened in Lacey's stomach every time she thought about TJ and Sally. Had she really done them any good by coming to Tyler Creek? Should she just be satisfied that they could do their figures and read a few books?

The children, including TJ, had just cleared out of the classroom. They would have a few minutes to enjoy the afternoon before a dress rehearsal for the play. Lacey was using the time to gather some of her personal items from the classroom and put them in a crate to take to the cottage. Some of the books she would leave; she had already decided that. Even on the peninsula, she could get new books more easily than most of these children could.

She gathered her lesson plans and a few pictures she had tacked to the walls. When the door creaked open, she was surprised that the children would be coming back in so soon. She struggled to take down a picture without tearing the corner.

"You may play a few more minutes if you like," she said, without turning around.

"I'm quite sure I've played enough," said a deep male voice.

Lacey spun around, flushed; the picture floated to the floor.

"Mr. Duncan," she said to the chairman of the school board. "What a pleasant surprise."

"I trust you've had a productive day," he said. "The children certainly look vivacious."

"They are quite excited about our end-of-the-year play. I'm sure they would be very pleased if you could attend."

"That's the day after tomorrow, isn't it?"

"Yes, that's correct."

"I'm afraid I'm due for a meeting in Paxton that afternoon. But I wish you well in your endeavor."

"Thank you. That's very kind to say."

Lacey had spoken to the chairman of the school board sporadically since she had arrived in Tyler Creek and usually it was in his office in Paxton. Why had he come to Tyler Creek today?

Mr. Duncan cleared his throat. "We've received quite complimentary reports on your performance from your co-teacher," he said.

"Maria is very kind."

"We have always found Miss Johnson's assessments to be reliable." He shuffled his feet and reached into his coat pocket for an envelope. "It is largely on her recommendation that I am pleased to offer you this contract."

Her hands shaking, Lacey reached for the document. "A contract?"

"For next year, with an option for the two years following that. We have received word that Victoria Stempel will be unable to return. Her health demands that she remain in the city near her doctor. The board discussed the situation at length. We see no need to begin a full-scale search for a new teacher when you have done such an admirable job. It's clear the children are smitten with you. A new teacher would have to begin again, whereas you would be able to build on the progress you've already made."

"I am very flattered, but I had not expected this," Lacey said. "My things are packed to go home."

"And go home you may. There is no need for you to stay here in the summer, if you do not wish to. We would welcome you back at the start of the new school year. I think you'll be pleased with the increase in salary."

Lacey could not focus on the words on the page in front of her. "I'm sure it's very generous."

"May I report to the school board that you are ready to take up the position on a permanent basis?"

Lacey swallowed. "Please do not think me ungrateful, Mr. Duncan," she said. "Your expression of confidence in my ability means a great deal to me. But I would like some time to think about the offer."

Mr. Duncan nodded. "Of course. You will want some time

to read over the details of the contract and make your needs known to the board."

"I'm sure the contract is fine."

"Perhaps we are mistaken in assuming you have not received another offer."

Lacey shook her head. "No, I don't have another offer. But when I accepted this position, it was temporary. I need some time to consider if it is the right position for me in the long term."

"Naturally. We will await word from you, then," Mr. Duncan said. "However, you will understand that we will need adequate time to recruit another teacher if you decide not to return."

"I will do my best to make a speedy decision," Lacey assured him. "I will send word before the end of June."

Mr. Duncan excused himself then and Lacey looked at the document in her hand. It was a contract that would allow her to teach the lower grades at the Tyler Creek school for another three years. Travis had challenged her to leave the peninsula for a few months and consider her calling. Had he expected this might happen?

As Mr. Duncan left, TJ slipped in through the open door. Lacey did not notice him at first. "Miss Wells?" he asked.

Lacey stared at the paper in her hand.

"Miss Wells?" he repeated as he walked quietly toward her.

Slowly, she looked up. "Yes, TJ? What do you need?"

"I know you're going away," he said, his voice quavering. "I wanted to tell you something first."

"Of course. What is it?"

"Before you came here, nobody every told me that I was God's business. I know God must be really busy, but it's still nice to think that I'm His business. I think He sent you here to tell me that."

"Oh, TJ, that's good of you to say." She reached out to stroke his face.

He blushed. "It's true."

Lacey nodded as tears pooled in her eyes. "Thank you, TJ."

"Miss Wells?"

"Yes?"

"I was wondering about the questions you had for God. Did He answer them?"

She swallowed hard and fingered the edge of the contract in her hand. "Some of them. And I'm sure He'll answer the others when it's time."

"Do you think it will be all right if I asked Him some questions?" TJ asked.

"Absolutely! Ask Him anything you want."

TJ shook his head. "No, I'm going to think of the most important questions, so I don't take up too much of His time."

"God has all the time in the world for you, TJ."

"I guess that's what it means to be somebody's business."

Once again the door opened. Patsy planted her feet and said firmly, "It's time to practice, Miss Wells. Are you ready?"

Lacey reached for a book and tucked the contract inside the front cover. "I'm ready!" she said enthusiastically. "Please tell the others it's time to begin."

eighteen

Coming through the clearing, Lacey drew in a deep breath of the sweet summer air, then she paused and leaned against her favorite tree. She was glad for a moment in her own clearing. Her weeks home on the peninsula had passed pleasantly. She had immediately resumed the late-night chats with her father on the tower's balcony, and confusion had tumbled out of her as she told her stories of Tyler Creek. Her questions remained, but she felt calmer for having talked about them.

Joel and Jeremiah treated her with new respect now that she was a "real" teacher. Micah, small for an eight year old, crawled into her lap at every opportunity and pleaded with her to teach him. Even her mother had changed and she no longer told Lacey what she ought to be doing all day long. But having lived on her own, Lacey no longer needed promptings to do what needed to be done.

Lacey had spent the morning with Abby, nearly eight months pregnant. Peter and Abby's house was sparsely furnished, but Abby appeared thoroughly satisfied with the progress they were making toward establishing a real home outside the lumber camp. Lacey had to admit the house was beautiful. Wood was easy to come by, obviously, and Peter had chosen well. As she walked through the house and let her fingers trail along the railings and bannisters, Lacey was momentarily envious of Abby for having a home of her own. Nevertheless, she had a difficult time picturing Travis doing the detailed carpentry work she saw all over the house.

Abby carried the baby well. Only twenty years old, she hardly slowed down with the growing weight. Her robust cheeks glowed in the golden summer sun and her eyes shone with a happiness that Lacey envied. Peter insisted, sensibly, that

Lacey should come to Abby rather than Abby walking to see Lacey. And Peter would not allow Abby anywhere near a horse.

During their visit, Abby had jabbered on about the new family. The owner of one of the mills who bought wood from the camp had decided to station a representative to make sure they got the best quality wood possible. The man, George Stanton, had a wife and small son. Peter and Travis, along with several others in the camp, were hastily putting up a house for the new family. Abby was thrilled to be getting neighbors so soon.

Lacey had been home for two weeks. The contract offered by Mr. Duncan lay on the top of her dresser, where she looked at it every day. She had promised him an answer by the end of June.

When she had arrived back on the peninsula, Lacey had showed the contract to Travis immediately. If he was going to give her a reason not to accept the offer, she wanted to know soon. Travis was pleased that she had received the contract and in front of her family retold the accounts he had heard of her work from Maria. Lacey listened carefully for any hint that he wanted her to stay on the peninsula. But none came. She had seen Travis several times, including that very morning and she had raised the subject of the contract. He said nothing. She pointed out it could be a three-year commitment, and still, he had said nothing. Instead, Lacey's compulsion to return to Tyler Creek grew steadily each day.

Yesterday, Lacey had sat up on the balcony of the light-house with her father. "You're not the same as you were," he had said, the breeze lifting his graying hair, which needed to be trimmed.

"How am I different?" she had asked.

"You have your calling now."

"Yes, I suppose I have."

"Your mother and I prayed every day that you would find your calling. . .and your peace."

"Mama prayed for me?"

"Why do you find that so surprising?"

Lacey shrugged. "I guess I shouldn't. I know her faith is real."

"Your mother has a tender heart," Daniel Wells said. "But she has had to adapt to life on the peninsula, and she has done so with a good spirit."

"When I went to Tyler Creek, I started to understand that. I had wanted to leave for so long. But Tyler Creek was not at all what I expected."

"Just as the peninsula was full of surprises for your mother." He turned to look at her. "You're going back, aren't you?" It was more a statement than a question.

"Yes, I believe I am."

"Even though it was not what you hoped for?"

"I don't know much about the voice of God, Papa. I don't hear words in quiet places; I don't have prophetic dreams; verses don't leap off the page when I read the Bible. But I think this is the right thing to do."

"Then you should do it."

They had sat in contented silence after that.

Lacey left her tree and headed out of the clearing. She would go home and sign the contract that afternoon. The acceptance letter could go with Gordon Wright next week, and Lacey would return to Tyler Creek at the end of August.

She could see her mother in the garden now. Mary Wells was hunched over the turnip patch, no doubt weeding and thinning as she went down the row. What had started as a small patch twenty-five years ago had grown to a plot that would provide vegetables for seven people all winter. Tending the garden was time consuming work and not always comfortable in the summer heat. Lacey determined to help tend her mother's garden through the summer and go back to Tyler Creek and harvest the vegetables she had planted there.

The twins would be off hunting rabbits this afternoon, Lacey knew, and Micah would have insisted on going with them. Joshua was out at the camp. Lacey and her mother could have a peaceful afternoon in the garden, and Lacey would find a way to tell her mother how she felt.

Mary Wells rose to her feet awkwardly and, with the back of one hand, she wiped her forehead wearily. For her, this was an unusual gesture and, even from a distance, she did not look right to her daughter. Lacey quickened her steps.

Suddenly, her mother lurched, lost her balance, and, with no attempt to right herself, slumped to the ground.

Lacey broke into a trot, screaming, "Mama! Mama!"

Sluggishly, Mary Wells rolled over and she struggled to her knees before collapsing again, face forward in the dirt in the middle of her garden and then she lay very still.

Keeping her eyes on her mother, Lacey stumbled over a root, took two steps to regain her balance, and then raced ahead. Finally, Lacey reached her mother and fell to the ground beside her.

"Mama? Mama, can you hear me?" Lacey pleaded.

Looking around, Lacey could see no reason for the collapse. Her mother had not tripped over anything. Lacey checked her mother for broken bones, and then she grasped her mother's shoulders and carefully rolled her over. In her mother's eyes was gratitude. . .and desperation.

"Mama, can you hear me?" Lacey repeated.

"Hear," Mary Wells said so softly that Lacey almost missed it. "Ca. . .ca. . .ta. . ." She seemed to choke on her own words.

"Mama, do you know where Papa is?" Lacey asked, scanning the yard. Then, at the top of her lungs, she screamed for her father as she pulled her mother to an upright sitting position. She felt the limpness in her mother's limbs as her body fell back against Lacy's chest.

"Ca. . .mmm. . ." Mary Wells said.

"It's okay, Mama, I'm here. Don't try to talk." Once again Lacey screamed for her father, who she realized must be up in the lighthouse and could not hear her above the wind. Still, she screamed.

"Mama, we're going to try to go to the house," Lacey said as she staggered to her feet, raising her mother's uncooperative body as she did so. She took a few tentative steps, stopped to regain her own balance, and then she stepped again.

"Lll. . .no. . .mmm."

"Just lean on me, Mama," Lacey said, knowing full well that her mother could do nothing else at that moment.

Lacey looked across the yard. They were more than fifty feet from the back door but, undaunted, she resumed the trek toward the house. Periodically, she stopped to readjust her mother's weight against her body and to call for her father. She looked toward the meadow; if only the boys would come home just now. Her mother grew heavier and heavier; her head sagged to one side. Lacey had never known her mother to admit to being sick even for a day. Even on the day Micah was born, Mary Wells was checking on her garden eight hours later.

At last Lacey reached the back porch and she sat on the step, cradling her mother's head and shoulders. "Papa!" she screamed. "Come! Now!"

Daniel Wells now thundered down the stairs and burst out of the bottom of the tower. His face paled at the tangled forms of his wife and daughter on the sagging wooden step.

"I found her in the garden," Lacey explained as he reached them. "I saw her collapse as I came out of the meadow."

"So it just happened?" he asked.

"Yes, just now."

He took his wife's face in his hands. "Mary? Mary?"

For a moment her eyes seemed to focus. "Da. . .Da. . . hhh. . ."

"I'm going for the doctor," he said resolutely. "It's a stroke, I'm sure of it."

"You'll be gone for hours!" Lacey said.

"I'll help you get her inside first," he said. "The boys should be back soon. You can send Jeremiah for Joshua before it gets dark."

With her father's help, her mother was soon laid out on her own bed, just off the kitchen. After a few more futile attempts to talk, she fell asleep. She had not moved a muscle by her own volition since she had collapsed in the garden.

"I've got to go," her father insisted. "I'll be back as soon as I can."

And he did go, leaving Lacey standing in the doorway and staring at the stranger on her mother's bed.

nineteen

Lacey shoved the window up as high as it would go but her effort made no difference. The air in the bedroom weighed thick and still, laden with humidity and lacking any breeze. On the bed, Mary Wells groaned under the thin sheet Lacey had tucked around her. The toes on her right foot twitched restlessly.

"Are you thirsty, Mama?" Lacey asked. Without waiting for a response, she poured water from the pitcher into a small cup and sat on the edge of the bed to offer it to her mother. Putting one hand firmly behind her mother's neck, Lacey helped her sit up enough to sip the water.

"Hhh. . .tt," her mother whispered. Then she swallowed awkwardly.

"Yes, it's hot," Lacey agreed. "It's the middle of July. The worst of the hot weather should be over soon."

Mary Wells's right leg kicked at the sheet.

"You have to stay covered," Lacey insisted as she tucked the sheet back in place. "The mosquitoes are terrible because of the wet spring. You'll get bitten up if we take the sheet off."

"Hhh. . .tt."

"Yes, it's hot. Let me sponge you off." Lacey dipped a cloth in a bowl of cool water and began wiping her mother's face. "Abby's baby will come soon. Peter wants a boy. Abby says she doesn't care, but I think she really wants a girl."

Mary Wells's eyes followed the motion of Lacey's hand as she moved the cloth to the basin and rung it out.

Three weeks had passed since Mary Wells's stroke in the garden and she was not better. Her right arm and leg moved freely, while her left side grew thinner every day with the lack of movement. The determined look in her eyes told Lacey that she understood every word that was spoken around her. More

119

than once, Lacey had chastised the boys for speaking in the room as if their mother could not hear what they said. But the best Mary Wells could say for herself were hoarse sounds, no real words. Lacey could only imagine the frustration welling up inside her mother.

Mary Wells might not ever be any better, the doctor had said when he finally reached the peninsula seven hours after her collapse. Daily exercises on the right side of her body might help her regain control of her muscles, and she could perhaps be helped to sit up in a chair for a few hours a day, but he did not think she would ever speak again.

"Will Mama die?" Micah had asked, his chin quivering.

The doctor had shrugged and looked over Micah's head at Daniel. "With good care, she should be comfortable and might be with you a long time. But we can't be sure of anything."

"So Mama won't ever be all right?" Micah persisted.

The doctor shook his head. "I'll try to come up and check on her from time to time," he said. "Be careful not to let bedsores develop, and do what you can to get her to eat."

"I'm going to pray that she will get better!" Micah declared.

The doctor laid his hand on Micah's head. "Only God can help your mother now."

Micah had slunk away to hide his tears. Lacey had seen his slender shoulders shaking.

Lacey's contract still lay on her dresser top, unsigned. She had prevailed upon the school board to give her a few more weeks to reach a decision because of the change in her personal circumstances. But she had not given up hope of returning to Tyler Creek. The boys could learn to manage Mama, and Daniel would have to take over lessons for Micah and the twins. Lacey had been sorting through her mother's boxes of lessons and books. She did not remember a time her father took part in her formal education, or Joshua's either. But he could guide Micah through a spelling lesson as well as anyone, Lacey was sure of that.

She squeezed out the rag and hung it on the side of the bowl.

her mother's eyes had closed. The air in the room was finally beginning to move. Then Lacey stole out to the kitchen, where Micah sat with a spelling list on the table in front of him. She leaned over his shoulder and looked at his work.

"I'm going to use my best penmanship," he announced, "so Mama will be proud. I'm going to write each word ten times, until I'm absolutely sure I can spell them perfectly."

"Mama will be proud, I'm sure. And when you've finished your spelling, you can do some arithmetic. I'll check it when I come back."

"Where are you going?"

"Travis is waiting for me. I won't be long."

"I'm going to finish before you get back."

"If Mama needs anything, you go tend to her, okay?" Lacey smiled and went out the back door.

Travis lounged on a bench along the side of the house. "This is the hottest day yet," he said, wiping sweat from his forehead. "I'm not sure I want to move."

Lacey reached for his hand. "There's a tree with some good shade on the other side of the chicken coop, but we may have to chase away the cow."

They strolled across the yard and settled onto the grass beneath the tree; shade had kept the ground cool. Before them, the tower looked over the cliff and, even from this distance, they could heard the water slopping over the rocks and lapping at the craggy cliff. On a windless day in the bright sunlight, it hardly seemed necessary to have a lighthouse at this location, but Lacey knew the terror that darkness and bad weather could bring. She pushed that thought out of her head and raised her face to the sun. At least the air up here was clean, not musty or sick smelling.

"You're doing a wonderful job," Travis said.

Lacey looked at him, a question in her eyes.

"I'm talking about the way you're holding the family together. I see what good care you are taking of your mother, and Micah is doing lessons, even in the summer."

Lacey sighed. "The twins haven't opened a book all summer. Mama would not be happy with that. When fall comes, Papa will have to insist that they get back to work."

"Are the boys all right?" Travis asked quietly. "I see Joshua quite often. He's concerned about your mother, of course, but he keeps to himself quite a bit. At least he's working and keeping busy. But the twins and Micah. . .are they all right?"

"It's hard to say. Jeremiah acts like nothing has changed. He spends all day tromping through the woods, doing who knows what. He has always had a mind of his own, and these days he gets to use it as much as he wants."

"And Joel?"

"He tags along with Jeremiah for lack of anything else to do. He doesn't seem to concentrate on anything. I don't think he cares if they ever catch a rabbit or not. And Micah, poor little Micah spends all his time doing things to make Mama proud. I'm sure she is proud, but he needs so badly to hear her say it, and she can't." Her voice was shaking. She stifled the torrent of words.

"Lacey, no one would blame you if you felt overwhelmed," Travis said quietly.

She shook her head. "There's no point in that."

Travis chuckled. "Now you sound like your mother. No time for feeling overwhelmed and discouraged, too much to be done."

"I'm beginning to think she was right all these years."

"What will happen in September?"

"Papa has talked to Joshua about cutting back on the time he spends at the lumber camp. If Joshua can come home a couple of times a week and help with chores, they'll manage. The twins are bright; they just have to be nagged into concentrating. The music lessons will have to stop, of course. Even Papa's patience won't extend that far."

"It sounds like you've thought everything through."

Lacey shrugged. "If Mama stays stable, it's only a question

of setting up a routine that all the boys can help with."

"So you will be going back to Tyler Creek without fail?"

Lacey turned and looked at Travis. His dark eyes met her gaze but betrayed nothing of what he was thinking. "I have not signed the contract yet," she said slowly. "If you think I should reconsider—"

Travis shook his head. "This is your decision, Lacey. I'll not stand in your way."

Lacey turned back to the water. "Travis, would it be so difficult to really tell me what you think, what you feel?"

He did not respond.

"I know my family needs me," Lacey continued, "but there is important work for me to do in Tyler Creek, as well. I have a calling to be there."

"I understand."

"Do you?" she said. "Do you really understand?"

"Of course. And I care about your happiness, Lacey Wells."

"Then why have you no opinion about what I ought to do?"

"Because this is your calling, not mine."

"And have you found yours. . .an educated city boy working in a lumber camp like a country bumpkin?"

Travis turned away, obviously stung by her words, and she wished she had not spoken them. "I'm sorry, Travis. That was unkind."

Travis stared across the yard. "Sometimes obedience takes you to strange places." He leaned toward her and nudged her with his shoulder. "You have ears to hear, Lacey. And you will hear God's voice when it is time."

Just then a shriek pierced the air. Travis jumped and looked around, but Lacey merely sighed. "That's Micah," she explained.

"It sounds like he's hurt," Travis said, alarmed.

Lacey shook her head. "Persecuted perhaps, but not seriously hurt. The twins must be back."

As she headed across the yard to sort out the disturbance, she wondered if she would recognize the voice of God so easily.

twenty

A few days later, Lacey sank into wooden chair in the kitchen, a towel in one hand and her apron half off. She could not believe what she had just heard Joshua say.

"You're leaving?" she echoed weakly.

"Leaving is the only way. If I stay I'll never reach my dream." Her brother sipped his thick hot coffee, calmly holding his ground. When had he started drinking coffee? He had become a man while she was away.

"Joshua, I don't know what you're talking about. I always thought you loved the peninsula. For the last two years, you've spent every moment you could working in the lumber camp."

"I do love it here, and I hope that I can come back someday. But it will be a long time."

"I don't understand."

"I want to study, Lacey. I want to go to college."

Lacey's jaw dropped. "If Mama were not so sick already, this would put her into shock. She always had to nag you about keeping up with your lessons. College?"

"Yes. I want to become a doctor."

"A doctor? Joshua, I had no idea."

"No one knows."

"What made you decide to do this?"

"Lumbering is dangerous work. I've seen a lot of accidents. Men have died because there was no doctor on the peninsula. And look what happened to Mama. Maybe if a doctor had been here sooner. . ."

Not a day went by that Lacey did not have the same thought. "Is that what you want to do. . .come back to the peninsula as a doctor?" she asked.

Joshua shrugged. "I think so. The peninsula is getting more

and more people every year, and we need a doctor here."

"What about the lighthouse?"

Joshua shook his head. "No, I'm not going to work the lighthouse. I outgrew that notion years ago."

"Have you told Papa that you're not interested in the lighthouse?"

"I think he knows. He makes comments about how much time I spend at the camp. Besides, he's not an old man. He doesn't need someone to take over yet. Also, he has three more sons."

"Ordinarily, I would agree with you, but taking care of Mama is going to wear him out. He's going to need help just to keep the household running smoothly."

Joshua looked down at his mug. "He keeps telling me how grateful he is for my help, now that Mama is sick. I didn't want to tell him I was leaving until I was sure."

"And you are sure now?"

"Absolutely."

Lacey could hear from his voice that Joshua meant what he said. "But Papa has a point, Joshua. The twins are only twelve. They can't do the heavy work that you can do. And what about Micah? Somebody has to pay some attention to him."

"Believe me, I've thought about all that." Joshua pushed his chair back. "But I have to go."

"Do you have to go now? Why not wait a couple of years? Joel and Jeremiah will be older." Frenzy rose within her.

"No, Lacey, I have to go now. The college has accepted me and they may not take me later. Or things will get worse around here and I'll never be able to leave. I can't put this off."

Lacey's throat tightened. She knew only too well how Joshua felt. "But Joshua, I'm due to go back to my teaching job in a few weeks. I can't ask the school board to indulge me any further. They must know if I am coming back."

"I know that," Joshua said quietly.

"Mama is so sick. The doctor doesn't think she's going to get better. She could be like this for years."

"I know that, too."

"We can't both go, Joshua." Lacey's fingers gripped the table.

Joshua was silent for a long time. He studied the coffee mug he held in both hands in his lap. Finally, he said, "I'm going, Lacey. I have to go, and I have to go now."

"Where does that leave me?" she cried out, nearly in tears.

"You have to make your own decision." His voice was soft but firm.

"What choice are you leaving me?" Her voice rose with fright and frustration.

Joshua raised his head now. "I'm not being selfish, Lacey. I'm doing what I think is best."

Lacey sighed heavily.

Micah burst through the back door. "Joshua," he said breathlessly. "Come, quick! There's a baby deer in the meadow."

Joshua glanced at Lacey and stood up. Tousling Micah's hair, he said, "Show me."

Micah tugged on Joshua's hand, unaware of any tension in the room, and Lacey marveled at his innocence, his pure pleasure in simple things. Alone in the kitchen, Lacey put her fingers to her temples and tried to rub away the headache that had overtaken her in the last few minutes. She sat in a stupor for a long time until she heard the weak moan coming from her mother's bedroom. She paused long enough to splash some water on her face before going to see her mother.

"What is it, Mama?" she asked gently as she stroked her mother's hair away from her face.

"H. . .t," her mother muttered as she thrashed in the tangled bedclothes.

Lacey stepped to the bedside and tugged on the sheet. Straightening it out, she tucked the end securely under the mattress and folded the top around her mother's waist. But her mother's good arm continued to beat against the bed.

"You're drenched," Lacey said. "You've perspired clear through your nightgown. I'll get you a fresh one."

Lacey selected the lightest nightgown her mother owned. In

the weeks since the stroke, she had learned how to manage her mother's lifeless weight without losing her own balance. Patiently and carefully, she changed her mother's gown. At last her mother lay back, content.

"Is that better now, Mama?" Lacey asked.

"Bos," she answered.

"The boys are fine, Mama. They went to the meadow with a kite and Micah found a new deer." She took her mother's hand. "Maybe soon you'll feel up to sitting in a chair near the window." Despite the optimism in Lacey's voice, she did not believe her mother would sit by the window.

"Bos," her mother said again.

"They'll be back soon, I'm sure. I'll send them in to see you," Lacey said as she sat on the edge of the bed.

"Dn. . .nl," her mother tried.

"Papa took the boat out to go get your medicine. Remember? He said good-bye before he left."

"Gd. . .gd," her mother echoed as she stared blankly at the ceiling. Then Lacey began to hum a hymn she knew her mother liked. At last the woman's eyes closed and her breathing steadied.

Lacey gently pulled her hand out of her mother's and returned to the kitchen. She had not been out of the house all day. Soon it would be time to start the stew for supper, and another day would be gone. Suddenly, the back door crashed open.

"I did not!" Jeremiah slammed through the doorway with Joel on his heels.

"You did, too! Don't lie to me!" Joel screamed, yanking on his twin's shirttail.

"Get your hands off of me. It's just a dumb kite."

"It was my kite." Joel shook his fist in Jeremiah's face. "And you crashed into that tree on purpose."

"I have no control over the wind. What did you expect me to do?"

"You didn't have to let it go so high." Joel shoved his twin.

Lacey jumped in. "Boys, boys, quiet! Mama's resting." And, to her amazement, they reduced their argument to pointed looks. "Are Joshua and Micah coming?" Lacey asked, glancing out the window.

"Who cares?" Joel said, stomping out of the room.

Lacey rolled her eyes. "What is going on with you two lately?" she asked Jeremiah. "It seems like you're always scrapping about something."

"It's Joel's fault. Everything little thing makes him mad."

Jeremiah was right. Joel was more sensitive than usual. Ever since their mother had fallen ill, he seemed on the verge of panic. A knock at the door interrupted her reflection. Jeremiah pulled it open.

"Hi, Travis," he said, then looked back over his shoulder at Lacey. "It's for you."

She jumped slightly and involuntarily straightened her skirt. "Travis! What are you doing here?"

He gave her a half-smile. "Aren't you glad to see me?"

She blushed. "Of course, I am." She met the gaze of his dark eyes.

"I had an errand on this side of the peninsula and thought maybe we could go for a little walk."

"An errand?" she said suspiciously. Unless Gordon Wright was due to arrive, and he was not, Lacey could not imagine an errand that would bring Travis to her.

"All right, so the errand is seeing you. It's a beautiful day."

"Oh, I can see that. And I would love a walk but I'm here with Mama. Papa's gone for a few hours. I don't think—"

"Oh, go on!" Jeremiah interjected from behind her. "You just said that Mama is resting. I promise to check on her in a few minutes."

"Are you sure, Jeremiah?"

"Don't you trust me?"

"Of course. It's not that—"

Travis chuckled. "Lacey, let's go before you dig yourself a deeper hole."

Lacey sighed. "Well, all right. I don't think we'll be long, Jeremiah. Mama probably won't need anything but some water. The heat's getting to her."

Travis took her hand and pulled her toward the door. To Lacey he seemed lighthearted and she was acutely aware of the difference between their moods. Her thoughts were a tangle of her mother's illness, Joshua's sudden news, and Joel's erratic behavior. She wanted to concentrate on being with Travis, but she could hardly put together a coherent thought.

"Lacey?" Travis asked.

"Yes?" She realized that she had not been listening to him. "I'm sorry, Travis. Can you say that again?"

"Never mind. It's not important." His eyebrows pushed together in concern. "Are you all right? Is your mother worse?"

Lacey shook her head. "No worse, no better. Just what the doctor said." She sighed and turned toward him. "It's not Mama, it's Joshua."

"Is he ill?"

"No. He's leaving." She recounted her conversation with her brother.

"So you're afraid you can't go back to teaching," Travis said.

"When I came home, I wasn't sure I wanted to go back. But I thought I was going to be able to make the decision. Then Mama got sick, now Joshua's news has come. The choice is being made for me. That's not supposed to happen."

Travis put an arm around her shoulders. "You're in a tough spot."

"It's impossible to make a choice that is best for everyone," Lacey continued. "I have to let the board know before it's too late for them to find a replacement. Gordon will be here any day. I have to send back a letter with him."

Travis stopped walking and steered Lacey around to face the other direction. "Let's go back, Lacey. I'd like to go up in the lighthouse."

"What for?" A moment ago she thought he was offering sympathy for her plight. Now he wanted to do something that made no sense.

"Just indulge me," he begged.

Travis led the way back and opened the small wooden door at the base of the tower. Lacey reached for the shelf just inside the doorway and found a candle. The winding staircase was engulfed in cool, musty air, the day's heat shut out by the thick stone walls of the tower.

"Ready?" she said softly.

"Lead the way," he said, and then she walked ahead of him up the tightly winding wooden stairs. The passageway was dark and dank and nothing like the outside of the lighthouse. The candle was for Travis's benefit for, after having spent her childhood climbing these stairs, Lacey knew every step.

Finally, they emerged into the light. Lacey started to go into the room that housed the great yellow light, but Travis touched her elbow. "This way," he said, nodding his head toward the door that would take them out to the narrow deck.

They stepped outside and stood side by side, resting their hands on the red railing. The air seemed cooler higher up, the breeze more refreshing. Lacey squinted into the sunlight that she had been oblivious to all day.

"Tell me what you see," Travis said.

Lacey balked. "The lake, the cliff."

Travis shook his head. "No, not just what you know is there. Take another look. For instance, look over there."

She turned her head to the left. "The meadow. There are so many trees on the peninsula, and in the middle of it all is that beautiful meadow. There's Joshua and Micah—and the deer! It's still there." Micah stroked the neck of the animal with the tender touch of a child.

"Keep going," Travis prodded gently.

"Micah has such a gentle spirit. Joel and Jeremiah don't understand him at all, but Joshua does. I think leaving Micah may be the hardest part of Joshua's departure."

"Now this way." Travis directed her gaze back to the water.

"I can't remember when I've seen the lake so blue," Lacey said. "When it's peaceful like this, it's hard to imagine how treacherous it can be during a storm or how lonely the winters are up here."

"Who made the lake?"

She turned toward Travis. "What are you talking about?"

"Just answer the question."

"God did."

"And Who made the cliff this lighthouse is built on?"

"God did."

"And Who keeps the cliff from sliding into the lake?"

"I suppose God does."

Travis swept his arm out over the lake. "You have a difficult decision to make, but you are not making it alone. For me, coming up here puts things in a different perspective."

"What do you mean?"

"The lake is treacherous and the winters are lonely. And everything you've ever said about the isolation of living up here is true. But somehow from this viewpoint, it doesn't seem so bad."

Lacey did not respond. Travis was not saying everything that was on his mind. A year ago, she had desperately wanted him to propose and take her away from the peninsula, but he had wisely made her see that getting married was no solution to her inner turmoil. She had come back matured but still sure she wanted to marry Travis Gates if he would ever propose. What was he waiting for?

She scanned the panorama that seemed to move him profoundly. His time on the peninsula was supposed to be brief, and already he had extended it twice. What was he hinting at—and did it include her?

twenty-one

The contract that had lain on Lacey's dresser for so many weeks was mailed back to Mr. Duncan, unsigned. With great regret, Lacey had explained, her personal circumstances would not allow her to resume teaching at Tyler Creek. Her careful lesson plans, written for TJ and Sally, Patsy and Maggie, Rebekah and the others, were stacked in a crate and tucked away behind barrels of fuel for the lamp.

Although not uncaring about the circumstances of his family, Joshua nevertheless was determined to go to college, and he left the peninsula during the first week of September, just as the heat of the summer was waning and the winds of winter were beginning to circle the rocks below the cliff. He promised to spend the long Christmas break at home but Lacey could not think that far ahead. She did not dream of Tyler Creek nor imagine how the routine would be easier when Joshua came home, for her hands were far too full keeping up with the work on the peninsula. She had no energy left to bemoan the fact that she had not returned to teach in a real classroom.

Lacey had picked the vegetables in her mother's meticulous garden and stood in the hot kitchen canning a supply that would last through the winter. Mary Wells ate less and less all the time and showed no pleasure when Lacey put bits of fresh vegetables in her mouth. But the rest of the family would be well-nourished because of Mary Wells's forethought.

Lacey's mind constantly contrived ways to keep her younger brothers constructively occupied. Joel and Jeremiah seemed to squabble less if they were expected to do something. Lessons had begun in earnest again, including piano lessons; the boys groaned but eventually cooperated, and for ninety minutes each day, one boy or another was at the keys. After a few weeks of allowing them to adjust to their mother's illness, Lacey continued to keep as much structure in the boys' lives as Mary Wells would have done herself, and they seemed to thrive.

Unfortunately, Daniel Wells retreated into silence much of the time. Robbed of the companionship of his wife of twenty-five years, he spent long hours at the top of the lighthouse, even in the summer when the water was safest. Despite her plans and schedules, Lacey could not imagine how her father would have managed the boys without her, even if Joshua were coming home every few days. Lacey was exhausted keeping up with it all.

Her mother was no better. To Lacey's keen eye, she seemed bonier and more listless with every passing day. Micah would sometimes sit at his mother's bedside, wordless and pale, and Lacey could find no words to comfort him.

Abby's baby had come in the middle of August after a torturous labor. Travis had come running for Lacey at the first sign of Abby's pain, and Lacey had sat with Abby and Mrs. Saget for nearly twenty-four hours. Finally, the baby came. Red-faced, Nathan Andrew squalled his first breath and was clearly afflicted with colic from the start. Abby insisted she enjoyed every moment of motherhood, but she was exhausted and it was cumbersome for her to visit Lacey with the baby. The two friends saw little of each other, and when they did, Nathan's bellowing made conversation impossible. Abby walked and jiggled him most of the day and deep into the night.

Two men at the camp were gravely injured in a logging accident, proving Joshua's point that the peninsula needed a doctor of its own, and several others had left in search of jobs in the city. With a shorthanded crew, everyone worked harder, including Travis, and Lacey had not seen him in nearly a month. On his first day off in weeks, Travis had borrowed a horse and came to take the boys hiking and promised to stay for supper.

With the boys out of the house for the afternoon, her father up in the light room, and her mother resting comfortably, Lacey had taken advantage of a moment to put her feet up. But it was only a moment, for she soon realized that she ought to be peeling potatoes for supper. Sighing, she pulled herself out of her mother's sagging but favorite chair and scuffled into the kitchen. She took a black iron pot off the wall and went outside to fill it with water.

It was not yet suppertime on a late summer day, yet the sky swirled with impending darkness. Lacey glanced off in the direction Travis had taken the boys, hoping that they were not too far away. She worked the pump until it began to spurt water, then set the pot under the flow. As she thrust her arm up and down, she surveyed the sky. A thick cloud cover had settled in over the lake. When she breathed, she took in the weight of the wet air. Lacey had no doubt that it would soon be raining and that this would be no ordinary rain storm. Spending her childhood in a lighthouse had made a weather watcher out of her.

Lacey heaved her pot back into the kitchen, lit the stove, and began peeling potatoes. She examined each one, pulling out stray spuds and the squirrelly growths that protruded from them. Potatoes grew plentifully in the yard and kept well in the celler, so the Wells family ate them frequently. As she began to peel them, Lacey speculated about how she might make them less ordinary for this one evening. But if she seasoned them creatively the boys would howl in protest, and if she failed to mash them she would have a difficult time feeding them to her mother.

Lacey took two potatoes and set them aside. Her mother would not eat more than a few bites anyway and there was no point in preparing a full serving of food for her any longer. She was so thin that Lacey had to steel herself to look at her, and her father's eyes hung in sorrow every time he sat with his wife who no longer seemed to know he was there. Micah had finally given up believing that his mother might some day recover.

Lacey checked on the meat, which had been simmering most of the afternoon. Some garden peas, fresh, not yet canned, and baking powder biscuits would round out the meal. Lacey pulled the lid off the flour barrel in the corner of the kitchen and reached deep inside. Gordon Wright was due to come with supplies the next day. If he did not bring flour, there would be no more biscuits for a time.

As she rolled out the biscuits, Lacey made a mental list of the chores for the next day. Micah was not as consistent as he ought to be in feeding the chickens, and the twins should learn to milk the cow without being reminded. Lacey kept hoping a bolt of responsibility would strike Joel and Jeremiah, and she would be spared having to remind them about every little thing. But, after having tromped through the woods all after-noon with Travis, they would be agitated and talkative and not of much use with the chores. Still, she was grateful that Travis was spending his free day with the boys. Lacey herself was focusing so much on structure that she sometimes forgot that the boys needed some fun.

Clapping her hands, Lacey let the flour dust settle into the sink before moving to the back door. The door had been propped open most of the afternoon to let the summer breeze roll through the house, but the breeze had now become a gale. The rain that had begun gently a few minutes ago was now steady enough to drench anyone caught in it. It was a bone-chilling rain, with enormous drops that slithered across every surface they touched.

The boys would be sopping wet by the time they got home, so Lacey went to the hall closet and removed a stack of towels. On her way back to the kitchen, she thought to check on her mother. Abruptly, she stopped as a burst of light flashed three times through the window. She waited a few seconds, and the signal came again. Her father was up in the light room, and he had given the signal for a ship to veer away from a hidden danger. Had he seen a ship, or was he being cautious in the storm?

Lacey began moving through the house again. The shutters rattled furiously in the wind, and she sighed thinking of the condition that the boys would be in. They ought to have come home by now. But perhaps they had taken shelter somewhere in the forest and would not be home in time for supper at all.

Back in the kitchen, she arranged the towels on a hook near the door. The sky was far too dark now. Instinctively, Lacey went to check on her mother who was awake, her eyes flashing from side to side as the house shook in the wind.

Lacey lowered herself into a chair at the side of the bed and kept perfectly still. *Does Mama hear something besides the wind?* she wondered as her mother's arm jerked awkwardly and she pleaded with Lacey with her eyes.

"Mama, what is it?" Lacey asked. "Is the wind troubling you?"

Still, Mary Wells's eyes flashed.

Then Lacey heard the sound of her father, calling from the tower. His full-throated cry was no match for the storm, but Mary Wells had heard it, and now Lacey heard it, hardly believing that it could sound so distant.

She dashed to the back door, flung a towel over her head, and threw herself out into the storm. With the wind pressing against her, she could do little other than bend her head and follow the side of the house to the tower door. Heaving with every ounce of strength, she pulled it open and hurtled inside. She did not stop to find a candle but pounded up the stairs toward her father's frantic voice.

twenty-two

Swollen from the dampness, the door at the top of the stairs did not want to open and, in pitch blackness, Lacey beat on it with her open hands. "Papa, the door!" she called, although she knew her father would not leave his post at the light.

Then Lacey heard him calling again very clearly now and, in a frenzied burst, she flung herself against the door as hard as she could. At last it gave way and she tumbled into the light room, where her father was gripping the light and swinging it in great circles. She blinked against the brightness of the four lamps burning brightly, their illumination multiplied in the reflectors behind them.

Lacey lurched over to her father. "I'm sorry I didn't come sooner," she shouted. "I didn't hear you calling."

"It's a large boat," Daniel Wells shouted over the raging storm. "I can't see what's happening. Go to the railing!"

Lacey left the shelter of the dome above the light and, in a few seconds, the towel on her head was drenched. As she scoured the churning waters below, she cast the towel aside and, with the sleeve of her blouse, she wiped the incessant flow of water away from her eyes. Not yet adjusted to the brightness of the light room, her pupils now rebelled against the darkness. Leaning over the railing, she tried to get her bearings. At first she saw no ship for the rain walled off the view in a solid sheath and whatever daylight was left was hidden deep behind the furious clouds, making it seem more like midnight instead of late afternoon.

Lightning split the sky and, in that instant, Lacey saw the craft. Her father was right: It was a large boat, not much bigger than the one Gordon Wright used to shuttle supplies back and forth. No doubt the owners had gone out on a routine errand on calm waters not knowing that the storm would come from nowhere with a ferocious surge that no one could have predicted. In a storm of this magnitude, with the wind blowing straight in toward the dock, there was little hope that such a lightweight boat would succeed in steering away from the rocks. The boat lurched toward the rocks while its crew worked frantically to change the position of the sail.

"Can you see it?" her father called. "Can you tell me which direction to look?"

"To the south!" Lacey shouted, choking on a mouthful of rain.

"The worst of the rocks are to the south," her father said as he simultaneously rotated the lamp southward and pulled on the rope that sounded the foghorn.

"More!" Lacey screamed over her shoulder. In the faint light, she saw three forms scurrying around on the boat's deck as the craft heaved with the motion of the water. Walls of water pounded the cliff and cascaded down over the treacherous rocks as the wooden boat tossed like a weightless piece of cotton.

Daniel Wells had done his job well. No craft had crashed against the peninsula in more than six years, although Lacey remembered many brutal fights against nature.

"Lord, be with those men!" she screamed, hardly hearing her own words. Gasping against the chill that now ran through her from head to toe, she scuttled back into the light room.

"How close are they?" her father demanded.

"Quite close," Lacey responded somberly. "I don't see how they will miss the rocks."

"If that boat hits even one rock, it will splinter into a thousand pieces," Daniel Wells said. "We should prepare to rescue the crew. Soneone must go down to the bottom of the ladder and throw out the white life rings with the longest ropes we have."

Lacey's chest heaved with the effort of standing out on the railing; for her to go down the ladder was almost unthinkable.

"Have your brothers come home?" Daniel Wells asked.

Lacey shook her wet head. "No, but I hope they took cover somewhere."

"We have no time to waste." Daniel Wells looked at his daughter. "Do you want to stay here and keep the light burning, or do you want to go down into the water?"

Lacey's heart lurched. She rarely went down the ladder, certainly not in a storm like this. But she would not send her father down, either. Besides, he was more skilled with the light than she was.

"I'll go down," she said, shivering, as she felt her way down the twisting staircase.

At the bottom of the stairs, hanging on hooks embedded in the brick, were two white rings tied to lengths of rope the thickness of Lacey's fist. The yards of rope were far heavier than she could manage comfortably, and so she determined that she would have to take one ring at a time. Grabbing one ring off its hook, Lacey bolted through the doorway and ran to the ladder as the rope unwound behind her. Finding the free end of the rope in darkness was difficult, but at last she had it in her hands. Repeating aloud the instructions for knots that she had learned as a child, she secured it to the crank that they used to haul supplies up the cliff. From the top of the cliff, she squatted and heaved the ringed end of the rope over the edge. It seemed forever before she heard the ring slap the water below.

Should she go for the other ring or clamor down the ladder to throw the secured ring farther out onto the water? Leaning over the edge of the cliff, Lacey peered into the blackness. *The light, Papa,* she pleaded silently, *swing the light.*

The light moved and she caught a glimpse of the boat that, miraculously, was holding its own so she scrambled back to the tower for the other ring and repeated the entire procedure.

Now it was time to for her to go down the ladder but her waterlogged boots were slowing her down. She grabbed at the laces and pulled the boots off. Then she scrambled down the ladder and crashed into the edge of the water. A wave nearly swept her off her feet but she held firm, and when it passed, she fished out the rings and prepared to throw them farther out.

She wished for a light of her own as she wondered if the crew would even see that she was throwing them a lifeline. She heaved the first white ring as hard as she could and it landed safely beyond the rocks; the second ring followed. She prayed they would catch a glimpse of the gleaming white forms.

Lacey waded back to the bottom of the ladder and with aching arms, clung to its security. Gasping for breath, she raised her eyes to the thrice-flashing light and heard the foghorn. Her father was doing everything he could. Lacey dared not leave her tenacious post until she knew whether she must haul in the ropes.

The hull of the boat heaved up and tilted precariously to one side, but the mast was still up and the sails caught the changing wind. The craft righted itself and veered away from the rocks. The storm continued to pound brutally, but the determined crew persistently moved the boat toward safety, a few inches at a time.

Not much farther, Lacey thought with growing relief. *Only a few more yards and you'll be clear.*

A few minutes later, confident that the boat would make it safely around the bend, Lacey climbed the ladder. Her father met her at the top with a dry blanket. Huddled together, they dashed toward the house and burst through the back doorway into the kitchen.

"My supper!" Lacey moaned, for she had not thought to dampen the fire in the stove before dashing to answer her father's call. The water had boiled out of the potato pot, and the meat that had simmered and filled the house with its aroma all afternoon was blackened and stuck to the bottom of the pan. The blanket slipped from her shoulders as she let both pans clatter into the sink. Dripping water puddled around her feet.

"Never mind the supper," her father said. "I'll check on your mother. Pray that the boys get back soon." He glanced out the window at the ferocious horizon.

Lacey stumbled across the hall to her own room, peeled off

her clothes, and snatched the quilt off her bed. Wrapped in it, she sat on the edge of the bed and shivered, too exhausted to move, too cold to rest. She heard her father's soothing tones telling her mother what had happened, and that all was safe.

Lacey had no idea what time it was, but hours must have passed since she had sat and peeled potatoes and regretted that she would have to mash them. As a vestige of daylight crowned the horizon, she became aware that the storm had abated and that the downpour had dissipated into a drizzle. Gradually, warmth came to her and her shivering slowed but her aching muscles demanded that she lie down. Still, Lacey was reluctant to shed her quilt and find some dry clothes.

Just then the back door swung open and Travis and the boys thundered into the house. "We got trapped," Joel announced loudly. "You wouldn't believe that storm!"

"Oh, yes, I would," Lacey heard her father answer. "Lacey and I were out in it ourselves."

"Lacey?" Travis asked.

"She was magnificent," Daniel Wells said proudly. "Fortunately the boat got through the passage safely, but Lacey was prepared for whatever might happen."

"She is a remarkable woman," Travis said so tenderly that Lacey almost did not hear the words. "She can always be trusted to do what must be done."

"I'm sorry that she couldn't go back to teaching," her father said in a low, almost sorrowful voice, "but I don't know what I would do without her right now."

Listening from her bedroom, Lacey threw off her quilt and reached for a warm, dry dress. Travis was right. She could do what needed to be done. And what was needed right then was a hot, filling meal for all of them.

twenty-three

Fall deepened steadily in the weeks after the storm. Gone were the summer showers that within a few minutes would cool the air and then dissipate into a mist. In their place came the graying skies of autumn and the hovering clouds that foretold of winter. Water crashed and swirled at the base of the cliff in the winds. Air blowing in off the cool lake chilled the house.

Lacey chided the boys to make sure they kept the door to the chicken coop closed and did not let the cow wander too far out into the meadow. Now Lacey kept one ear cocked for her father's voice all the time; he seemed in a heightened state of watchfulness, spending hours on end up in the lighthouse. Lacey heard the fog horn blow at every hint of a gray sky and she knew it would soon be time to batten down for the winter, when crossing the peninsula even with a horse and cart would turn cumbersome.

The Wellses would be on their own for the winter, afternoon visits with Abby would cease, and Travis would have to forego Sunday dinners with them. Lacey sighed as she thought of the loneliness that winter always brought but, in reality, it mattered little to her routine. Keeping up with schooling the boys, nursing her mother, and running the household left her very little time for visiting with a childhood friend or wondering about the intentions of a charming young man. Lacey did not know if her mother had always been so harsh as she had seemed in the last few years, but her own eyes were opened to the consuming reality of forging a life for a family in this place. Even as Mary Wells lay still in her bed, Lacey's appreciation for her mother's tenacity grew every day. Mary Wells had stopped perspiring and started shivering, and now it seemed that Lacey could not keep her warm enough. Every morning and every afternoon,

142

Lacey forced herself to be cheerful as she entered her mother's room and worked the lifeless limbs. She had long ago given up hope that the habit would have any true therapeutic value; Lacey knew her mother would never again move her left side voluntarily. But the forced exercise seemed to help with the bedsores and encouraged her mother to move the right side of her body, even if in protest of the entire procedure.

"She seems no worse today," Daniel Wells had taken up saying. He woke beside his wife in the mornings and spoke to her gently as he readied himself for his day. "I believe she's holding her own now."

Lacey agreed with her father's assessment that her mother did seem to be holding her own. She was not getting worse; but she was not getting better. Her eyes would follow Lacey around the room as she tidied and cracked the window for fresh air but she no longer spoke, and she slept for longer and longer stretches of time.

Even Micah, who had clung to his hope longer than anyone else, had given up believing that his mother would recover. He faithfully visited with her several times each day, and she seemed to appreciate it, but Micah knew his mother would not get better. With his belief had also gone his dedication to his lessons, and Lacey had to nag him almost as much as she did Joel and Jeremiah.

Today was no different. Lacey sat in her mother's easy chair with her head back, listening to Micah read. She dared not close her eyes for fear that she would lose concentration completely and be of no help the next time Micah encountered an intimidating word. As it was, she did not immediately notice when Micah stopped reading. She blinked herself to alertness and urged him on.

"I don't want to read any more," Micah whined. "The twins have already gone to play."

"They finished their lessons," Lacey reminded him. "You have only a few more paragraphs and you'll be finished with this chapter."

"But I don't want to finish it. I want to leave it until tomorrow." He slapped the book shut.

Lacey was too weary to argue further. "All right, but you must make up the time tomorrow. Ten extra minutes."

"I'm going out to look for deer." Micah grabbed his jacket and was out the door.

Now Lacey closed her eyes. The clock on the sitting room wall ticked, but otherwise, the house was silent. Mary Wells was sleeping, the boys were all outside, and Daniel Wells was in the tower, polishing the reflecting glasses and the brass trim. Lacey thought of the pile of clothes that needed to be washed, but she lacked the energy to pump enough water to begin the job. It would have to wait another day, even if it meant that Micah wore a dirty shirt tomorrow.

The door creaked open and Lacey heard Micah's footsteps crossing the kitchen. "Did you change your mind?" Lacey called out.

Another set of footsteps followed Micah's.

"Joel? Jeremiah?" Lacey said.

Micah grinned as he appeared under the archway that set off the sitting room. "Look who I found."

Lacey reluctantly opened one eye and then the other more rapidly. Instantly alert, she jumped out of her chair. "Travis! I wasn't expecting you today."

"I know," he said quietly.

Something in his manner struck Lacey odd. His face looked worn out. "What's wrong? Is it Abby?" Lacey asked.

Travis glanced at Micah and Lacey turned to the eight year old. "Did you find a deer, Micah?"

He shook his head. "I just found Travis."

"Then why don't you keep looking," she suggested.

With no further prompting, Micah turned and left the room. When she heard the back door swing closed behind him, Lacey repeated her question to Travis.

"No, Abby is fine and Peter and Nathan are fine."

"Then what is it? You look like you've lost your best friend."

"That just might be the case." His eyes would not meet hers.

Lacey moved around to try to capture his gaze. She put one hand on his arm. "Travis, what are you talking about?"

"I came to say good-bye, Lacey," he said quietly, not raising his eyes.

"Good-bye?" she echoed.

"Yes. I'm leaving the peninsula."

"When?"

"Today. Gordon should be here with his boat in a few minutes."

Lacey withdrew her hand. "Then you must have arranged this weeks ago."

Slowly Travis nodded. "Gordon says I must go now or I may not have another chance until spring."

"Are you so anxious to go that you cannot wait until spring?" Lacey failed to control the quiver in her voice.

"I have stayed far longer than I expected to already."

"That's true. It's been a year and a half."

"It was only supposed to be a few months."

"Yes, I remember."

"And now I must go."

"But, why? Why now?"

"It is time."

Lacey sat down on the edge of a chair. She had hardly seen Travis in the last few weeks, but knowing that he was only a few miles away on the other side of the peninsula had somehow comforted her.

"Where will you go?" she asked.

"Home," he answered hoarsely.

"I thought the peninsula was your home now."

"To my father's home."

"Is he unwell?"

"Not to my knowledge. But he does want me to return."

Lacey knew very little about Travis's father. Travis rarely spoke of him, and when he did it was in vague terms with little emotion. She found it difficult to believe that such a distant relationship was compelling Travis to leave the peninsula, but she had no right to ask further questions. Travis had never promised her anything, and she was wrong to take anything for granted.

Lacey's eyes moved to the window. Micah roamed the yard beyond the glass. "Micah will be devastated," she said softly. "He has become quite fond of you."

"And I am fond of him," Travis responded, also looking out the window. "I'll try to explain it to him on my way out."

"He's going to have questions."

"I know."

They stood side by side at the window, and Lacey could feel the heat from his body warming the air around her. His breathing seemed weighted and his posture strangely stiff, but he kept his hands in his pocket and his gaze forward.

"Travis, do you. . .will you. . .?" Lacey tried to speak.

Travis shrugged. "I can't tell you any more, Lacey. I'd better go on down. I promised Gordon I wouldn't keep him waiting when he gets here."

He turned and retraced his steps to the back door. There he picked up a bag before crossing the yard to where Micah played. Micah grinned in greeting, but his expression sobered when Travis lowered himself to Micah's level and spoke earnestly. Lacey watched from the kitchen. Travis had avoided looking her in the eye, but he locked his gaze with Micah's and spoke briefly. Confusion crossed the little boy's face, and he turned and looked over his shoulder toward the cliff.

Lacey saw her brother's mouth move. He was asking a string of questions. She could easily imagine what they were, because she had not had the courage to ask the same questions lurking in her own heart.

Travis pulled himself to his full height, picked up his bag, and began walking toward the rope ladder that would take him down to the water's edge. Before disappearing over the edge, he turned and waved at Micah and turned his eyes to the window where Lacey still stood. And then he was gone.

Micah burst into tears.

On the dock below, Travis greeted the incoming craft of Gordon Wright. "Did you tell the little lady farewell?" Gordon asked in his usual brusque manner. "Won't she even come to see you off?"

Travis threw his bag on the deck and boarded the boat without comment.

"You didn't tell her why you're leaving, did you?" Gordon said.

Travis shook his head.

Gordon scoffed. "She's a smart wench. She just might understand if you told her what you were up to."

Travis still said nothing and, as Gordon pushed off, he stared at the lighthouse and wished he had climbed its tower one last time.

twenty-four

Two brown-haired and one blond one bent over the dining room table. Joel and Jeremiah had each plowed their way, under protest, through a Dickens novel and were now in the throes of the written reports that would prove they had followed the story accurately. The final version must be completed before they could leave the table for the day.

Micah was struggling with his arithmetic. Lacey had written out a page of addition and subtraction that required him to borrow and carry his totals, and Micah did not like it.

Lacey sat at the end of the table, trying to darn a wool sock. She had learned many things from her mother, but she had never mastered darning neatly. She took out her most recent stitches and started again. Winter had set in. The first snow of several inches was already on the ground in mid-November. The boys would need all the wool socks she could salvage.

Joel leaned over and looked at Jeremiah's paper. Jeremiah responded by heaving his shoulder into Joel's chest.

"Hey!" Joel protested.

"Mind your own business," Jeremiah answered.

"I just wanted to see how far you are."

"You're going to steal my ideas."

"We didn't even read the same book."

"Boys, please," Lacey pleaded as she set the sock aside. "He started it!" Jeremiah declared.

"All I did was look," Joel said in his own defense. He had one hand clasped over his injured chest.

"I don't want to hear about it," Lacey said. "I was sitting right here. Just finish your reports and you can go your separate ways."

The twins were twelve years old but ever since their mother had fallen ill, they behaved as if they were five. In fact, everyone acted differently. Joel and Jeremiah were determined to test the extent of Lacey's new authority over them, even if it meant bringing physical harm to themselves. Micah no longer reveled in every detail of nature and, now when he went outside, he wandered aimlessly around the yard and could report very little when he returned. And her father, never a man of many words, said even less.

Micah slumped back in his chair. "I can't do this," he whined. "I don't understand. How can I take nine from zero."

"Impossible," spouted Joel.

"Can't be done," agreed Jeremiah.

Lacey narrowed her eyes at them. Immediately they turned their heads back to their papers. She turned to Micah. "You're not taking nine from zero," she explained for the fifth time that day. "You're taking nineteen from thirty." Once again she showed him how to borrow and take nine from ten instead of zero. "Now, you try it on the next one." She handed the pen back to him.

Micah took it, but he lowered his hands to his lap instead of the paper. "Another thing I don't understand is why Travis left. Doesn't he love us anymore?"

Lacey picked up the sock and twisted it between her fingers. "I'm sure Travis had a very good reason for going," she said. "He meant to visit the peninsula for only a few months."

"Why did he visit so long, if he didn't like it here?"

"He loved it here," Lacey said quietly. "Back to your figures, please."

Micah did one problem. "It's just not the same without Travis around."

"He was hardly ever here," Jeremiah pointed out, "and he came only to see Lacey, anyway."

Alarmed, Micah turned to his sister. "Is that true?"

Lacey glared at Jeremiah. "Travis is very fond of you, Micah. I know he always looked forward to seeing you."

"Travis wouldn't make me do these dumb sums," Micah muttered.

"Oh, yes, he would! Travis's father is a businessman. I know he made sure Travis could take nineteen from thirty."

"Well, I'm not going to be a businessman. I'm going to operate the lighthouse."

"You still have to be able to figure or you'll never know if Gordon is bringing you the right amount of fuel." She thumped his paper. "Finish, please. I'm going to check on Mama. I'll be right back."

In her parents' bedroom, Lacey found her father sitting at the side of the bed. The curtains were drawn, leaving the room in a dusky shadow. "Papa?" Lacey said quietly.

As if in slow motion, his head turned toward her. He did not speak.

"Papa, are you all right?" she asked.

He nodded, then shook his head.

"Papa, what's wrong?"

"Look at her. I don't think she even knows I'm here today."

Lacey touched her mother's shoulder; her mother's eyes fluttered open and immediately closed.

"She sleeps all the time," her father said. "She's so thin. She doesn't talk."

"I think she knows when you come," Lacey said. "She always seems better after you stop in during the day."

Her father shook his head adamantly. "I used to think that but not anymore."

Lacey did not know what to say.

"You would have liked your mother," he said.

"What do you mean, Papa? You know that I love Mama, despite all our differences."

"It's this place," he said. "If you could have known her somewhere else, when she was young, you would have enjoyed her. When I met her, she was a light. . .a brilliant lamp. I had not known many young women, but I knew that Mary Cooper was miles ahead of the rest. But I brought her here and she did what she had to do to survive."

"Papa," Lacey said, unsure what she would say next. "It takes a remarkable woman to do what Mama did. I don't think she is sorry about anything."

"She would never let us know," he said. "But what if I had not brought her here. I could have stayed in the city. If she hadn't had such a harsh life. . .if there had been a hospital here. . ."

Lacey sat on the edge of the bed and took her father's hand. Daniel Wells was the last person on earth she would expect to have any doubts about how he had lived his life. Yet, here he was, wondering about how things might have been different.

He looked at the drawn curtains. "You mother's sister gave us those curtains twelve years ago," he said.

"I remember."

"They have never fit the window properly, and they were faded along the edges when we got them. But your mother never complained."

Lacey said nothing.

"Your mother deserved better than a life of hand-me-down curtains and inadequate supplies of flour. And now look what I've done."

"She's not sorry, Papa. She wanted to be with you."

"She had never been to the peninsula before she agreed to marry me."

He put his head in his hands and Lacey did not know what more to say. "Can I do something for you, Papa?" she asked.

He shook his head. "I'll just sit here a while longer, then I'll get you some wood for the stove."

Lacey quietly moved to the kitchen for it was time to start supper. She would make some biscuits to go with the ham and bring up a jar of green beans from the cellar. Taking a mixing bowl with her, she went to the barrel in the corner and measured out enough flour for the biscuits. Outside, flecks of snow swirled through the air, threatening to leave a fresh coat on the ground.

Lacey recalled the previous November. She was two months into her temporary teaching job in Tyler Creek and expected that Travis would propose any day. They could marry when she finished her contract, she had thought, and go to the city to pursue Travis's business interests with his father.

Such speculation had belonged to another person, Lacey now thought. She had returned to the peninsula and might not leave again for a very long time. Travis had sent no word since his abrupt departure, and Lacey was realistic enough to know that she might never hear from him again. But she dared not be as brazen with her feelings as Micah was. She had no time for daydreaming in the meadow or girlish imaginings with a childhood friend. She had her mother to care for and the boys to look after. And now her father. In all her twenty years, Lacey had never seen Daniel Wells in such a frame of mind. Lacey had grown up under the shadow of her father's calling to tend the light. For him, running the lighthouse was not a job, not a responsibility, it was a passion woven into the way he viewed life itself.

When Lacey had entered adolescence, she and her father had begun their occasional talks along the railing. What does it mean to have a calling? How does God call His children? How would Lacey know she was making the right decisions for her future? Lacey still struggled with those questions. But Daniel Wells was her touchstone for finding answers. To hear her father say he regretted bringing his bride to this place was almost more than Lacey could comprehend. What grief, what emptiness would drive him to say something like that?

"Lacey?" Micah called from the dining room.

"Coming." Leaving her bowl of flour on the table, Lacey returned to the dining room. The twins were gone, but their book reports were there.

"Can I go now, too?" Micah asked.

Lacey picked up his paper and scanned over his answers. She circled two of them. "You'll have to do these again," she said.

Micah groaned and Lacey sighed.

twenty-five

Lacey shivered and the shivering wrenched its way into uncontrolled quaking. She clenched her jaw and tried to stop but the shaking welled up inside her, bursting for its freedom through her teeth. Cold air shimmied through her coat and chilled the dress she wore underneath. Her only black dress was a thin one, not at all suitable for a wintery funeral the day after Thanksgiving.

Two days earlier, Daniel Wells had come back from his early morning rounds of stoking the stove and checking on the animals to find his wife oddly still but with her eyes wide open. Her mouth, too, looked as if she had been trying to call out. A few minutes later, Lacey had found her father slumped against the side of the bed and she knew that her mother was gone.

Micah had shrieked at the news and had wailed his way through the next two days. Lacey held him and rocked him as he trembled. She was twenty years old, Joshua was on his own, the twins were nearly teenagers and they had all benefitted from the firm but dedicated mothering of Mary Wells. But Micah was an eight-year-old child who needed his mother and would never have her again. As Lacey sought to comfort Micah, she felt as helpless as she had when trying to help TJ Richards and no explanation seemed good enough for what had happened and no alternative for the future would be as good as the past.

The twins had turned quiet, as had Micah. They pushed away their breakfast plates with the news and hardly touched the food Lacey offered to them since then. The pies she had hoarded for Thanksgiving were still on the shelves in the cellar. She had cooked the butchered turkey, but no one wanted any of its meat.

153

And now they stood gathered around their mother's casket. Lacey was relieved it was not a sunny day. She could not have stood seeing the landscape sparkle on the day she buried her mother. The gray sky supported the mood of the morning. Micah clung to her side with his face buried in her waist. He had not wanted to come to this final farewell, but his father was afraid that Micah would regret his choice later and insisted that Micah attend the funeral. Joshua was missing. They had tried to send word immediately, of course, through a lumberjack who was willing to travel the land route to a place with a telegraph. But they had no way to know if the message had reached Joshua, and it would likely take him two days to get home once he heard the news. Lacey did not expect him before Christmas.

Lacey had trudged over to the lumber camp on Wednesday afternoon to tell Abby's family the news. The path was icy and Lacey had declined to take the horse and cart because she trusted her own footing more on the uneven path frosted and blanketed by the snow. The trek had taken her nearly three times as long as it did in fair weather, and she was chilled to the bone when she arrived at Abby's tidy little house.

As soon as Abby saw her friend, she knew what had happened. Maternally, she seated Lacey in the chair near the open fireplace and brought her a thick quilt to replace her damp coat. Lacey was vaguely aware that Nathan was fussing in the background.

Abby's mother, the only female friend to Mary Wells on the peninsula in the last twenty-five years, stifled her sobs and went immediately to her kitchen. At points of crisis, cooking was what she did best.

Peter, Abby's husband, returned immediately with Lacey and helped Daniel Wells build a solid casket. He brought his horse and pulled a cart with a selection of fine wood. Abby's father, manager of the lumber camp, insisted that Mary Wells would not be dumped in the ground in a slapped together pine box. On Thursday Abby's father joined Daniel Wells and Peter to dig a hole in the frozen earth. The icy ground had resisted their efforts, mocking their shovels and splintering beneath their blades only after great effort had been exerted. Mary Wells would be laid to rest next to Daniel Wells's parents, who had also tended the light.

Lacey had not come to the family plot for years. As a child she had played there and wondered about the names and dates she saw etched in the stones. But she had never pictured anyone from her family there.

The gathering at the funeral was small by city standards but overwhelming by the measure of the peninsula. Tom Saget had closed the mill and many of the men who respected Daniel Wells made their way over to pay their last respects.

No minister came, of course. Daniel stood before the crowd in the black suit he had been married in twenty-five years earlier. He refused to wear an overcoat and Lacey marveled that the cold seemed not to bother him. As he shuffled and cleared his throat, Micah squeezed Lacey's hand nervously.

"Mary was a woman of faith. She went rejoicing to her Savior. I won't lie to you. I'm sorry she's gone. I'm sorry she was so ill for her last months on earth. I don't know why that happened. But she's with the Lord now, and we must give thanks for that."

A few of the mourners murmured their amens to Daniel Wells's sentiment.

"The boys are going to play," he explained, "and I hope you will all join me in repeating Psalm Twenty-three."

Joel picked up his violin and Jeremiah straddled his cello. Lacey swallowed a sob at the memory of all the music lessons Mary Wells had given the twins. Surely, she had not imagined that they, at the age of twelve, would be playing at her funeral.

After a hesitant start, they played steadily through four verses of "Amazing Grace" and Lacey pictured her mother, keeping time with a knitting needle against the edge of the dining room table. Their last notes drifted into the wind, and

Daniel Wells stepped forward again.

" 'The Lord is my shepherd,' " he said quietly, " 'I shall not want.' "

The others joined in and Lacey moved her mouth, but somehow the sounds would not come.

" 'And I will dwell in the house of the Lord for ever,' " Daniel Wells finished. He cleared his throat again. "The women have prepared some food. You are all welcome to come to the house and warm up before going your ways."

Awkwardly, a funeral party dominated by lumberjacks trailed over the ridge and toward the house. The turkey would soon be consumed. Abby and her mother had baked bread and cakes to go with the pies in the cellar. Lacey was not sure how all these people were going to fit in the tiny house at one time. But they must be warmed and fed before crossing the peninsula again.

Once back at the house, Abby promptly handed Nathan to Peter and assumed the role of hostess. She insisted that Lacey situate herself in the sitting room among the guests and let her and her mother take care of serving food and steaming coffee.

Peter roamed the room easily with Nathan on his hip. At three months Nathan was far less fussy than he was as a newborn, and Peter seemed quiet comfortable caring for him. Lacey admired that. No matter who Peter was talking to, and he talked to everyone, when Abby flitted through the room with a fresh tray of sandwiches, he raised his eyes to catch her glance. Each time a smile traced Abby's lips.

Lacey had to admit that Abby seemed supremely happy. When she had announced her engagement to Peter, Lacey's spirit had sunk with the conviction that her dear friend was settling for second best. To marry a lumberjack and have a string of babies while trapped on the peninsula had seemed a dismal future to Lacey. But Abby was thriving. Her eyes never lost their shine, a colicky baby had not ruffled her nerves, she embraced a pioneer spirit and built a real house in the midst of a lumber camp. Lacey had to admire her friend. Abby had made a choice that Lacey was sure would mean she was trapped, but Abby did not look trapped now. She looked happy.

Lacey was the one who felt trapped. She had passed up the opportunity to return to Tyler Creek, and not a day had passed that she did not think of TJ and Sally and wonder if there was something more she could have done to help them. And would anyone ever care enough to help them?

Abby's mother drifted by with a tray of small cakes. "Your mother would have been happy with the service, don't you think?" she said.

Lacey nodded. "She would have been proud of the twins."

"She taught them well. I only hope Nathan will have as good a teacher someday." She drifted off again.

Micah appeared at Lacey's side. His eyes drooped and his shoulders sagged. "Did you have something to eat?" Lacey asked him.

He shook his head.

"If I fix you a plate, will you eat it?"

Again he shook his head.

Lacey sighed and opened her arms. Micah immediately clamored into her lap and snuggled against her chest. Even at eight, he was able to curl into a tight ball and hold very still. His shoulders rose and fell with his breathing. Lacey stroked the top of his head.

Father, she thought, *is this the child You want me to help? Show me what to do.*

twenty-six

Examining the rag, Lacey determined that she would soon need a fresh one. The brass trim on the glass case enclosing the light had been neglected in the weeks of her mother's illness. Soot had accumulated everywhere, and Lacey had finally decided to tackle the job.

Normally, Daniel Wells was meticulous about this task and he polished spots that no one else saw. Certainly no one in the waters below could detect the smudges he refused to tolerate. Under his supervision, all of the Wells children had learned to scrub and polish even the parts that already gleamed in the sunlight.

But Daniel Wells had lost his spark; his wife's illness had shaken him enough that he slowed down. In the fall he had been of little help to Lacey in harvesting the garden. Instead, she had conscripted the boys to pick vegetables and help with the canning. With every week that passed, he did less; now he expended effort only for what absolutely could be ignored no longer. Lacey was horrified to think how the family would have fared had she returned to Tyler Creek. Even Joshua might have stayed home had he seen his father in such a state. Joshua would be home in two more weeks for Christmas. He would see for himself.

Daniel Wells made routine visits to the tower throughout the day, but he did not stay long. Lacey was used to her father spending hours in the peaceful tower if there were no other demands on his time. After the funeral, she had expected that he might spend even more time in his private refuge. But the tower did not beckon as it had for all those years. Now he was more likely to sit in a rickety wooden chair in the backyard. In a matter of just a few weeks, he had turned into an old man.

Lacey rubbed harder with the cloth. It was cold in the tower and she had to keep moving to keep warm. The wind swirled around the tower and whisked through the light room. If she stopped for very long, her fingers might go numb.

At one point she leaned over the railing and surveyed the yard, hoping that the boys were behaving themselves. She had heard no shrieks of terror from Micah. The twins were supposed to be stacking wood near the back door so they would not be caught short if a blizzard struck. Lacey found herself following all the precautionary patterns of her mother. The flour barrel was kept full, jars of vegetables were neatly stacked in the cellar, meat was hung to dry for jerky. If winter assaulted with full blast, the Wells family would be prepared.

Movement in the water caught Lacey's eyes. A small craft had rounded the jutting land and seemed headed for their dock. Lacey followed her curiosity and peered down at it. It was Gordon Wright's boat. He had come several weeks ago with extra portions of provisions and a stern warning about the need to ration them carefully. She had not expected to see him for several more weeks, until the worst of the winter was over. Lacey thought it remarkable that he had managed to navigate the choppy water, but there he was. Even more remarkable, Gordon was not alone. A second figure now stirred on the deck of the boat. As Gordon wrestled with the sails to turn the boat toward the dock, Lacey's heart thumped faster. The brown hair was longer and the beard was new, but the second figure was too similar to Travis not to be him. Forgetting the cold, Lacey stared down. The figure raised his face to Lacey and then a hand. Yes, it was Travis.

Why did he not sent word he was coming? she wondered. But, of course, no one had brought news from the southern part of the state in weeks. Lacey was not even sure if Joshua had received news of their mother's death. A greater question was why Travis was returning at all. Two months ago, on the day of his departure, he had made no promises to return. He had left Micah, and Lacey, tormented by his departure with no hint that it might be temporary. Why had he come now?

The boys had seen the boat now and were peering over the cliff at the dock. Micah squealed and waved in delight. Lacey winced as she saw him lean farther over the edge than he should have. Jeremiah sensibly pulled him back. Lacey instinctively lurched for the stairs and started her descent. By the time she reached the bottom of the tower and emerged into the sunlight, the boat was docked and Travis was getting off. Gordon waved up at her and she returned the gesture.

"It's not too wicked a day for a boat ride," he challenged her. "Bring a blanket, and we'll head for the lake."

Lacey rolled her eyes. Gordon was nothing if not persistent. But he was already preparing to leave, having discharged his cargo.

"Have you brought no provisions?" Lacey called down.

Gordon spat and shook his head. "I told you the last time that you'll have to be careful in the winter. Your mother always has been."

Travis turned and gave the boat a shove. Gordon waved his farewell and Travis began to climb the rope ladder, dragging an overstuffed bag behind him.

"I knew you'd come back! I knew you'd come back!" Micah cried, jumping up and down.

Lacey stood protectively behind Micah, keeping just enough weight on his shoulder to keep him from doing something rash. In another moment, Travis's head appeared at the top of the ladder and her eyes met his gaze over the top of Micah's head. She had both hands pressing quite firmly on Micah's shoulders but he wriggled for his freedom. As Travis emerged from the ladder and tossed his bag to one side, Micah hurtled toward him and jumped into his arms. Lacey had not seen such liveliness in her little brother since well before their mother's death.

"I just knew you couldn't stay away," Micah exclaimed. "No one believed me, but I knew."

Travis smiled. "And you were right, weren't you?" He

smiled at Lacey. "Hello, Lacey."

Jeremiah tugged on Micah's leg. "Come on, let's go."

"Go where?" Micah asked.

Jeremiah glanced at Lacey. "Just come with me. I've got a project for you."

Micah slid down Travis's torso and thumped to the ground. "What is it?" he asked.

Jeremiah rolled his eyes. "Just come with me and find out."

Micah turned to Travis. "You'll be here when I get back?"

Travis smiled and nodded. "You go with Jeremiah. I'll talk to you later."

Lacey threw a grateful and nervous glance at Jeremiah. When the boys were gone, she turned toward Travis.

"Hello, Lacey," he repeated.

"Hello, Travis." Questions pelleted her mind, but she did not ask them.

"You are a sight for sore eyes," he said.

She smiled. "Is that really you behind that beard?"

He chuckled and stroked his hairy chin. "It's me. Do you like it?"

Lacey nodded. "I didn't know you were coming back."

"No one did."

"How did you persuade Gordon to bring you, especially at this time of year?"

"Let's just say I impressed upon him the urgency of my voyage."

"And what was so urgent?"

Travis glanced out over the water. "Unfinished business."

Lacey nodded, even though she did not understand.

"How is your mother?" he asked.

Lacey sucked back a gasp. "I thought Gordon would have told you."

"Told me what?"

"Mama died just before Thanksgiving."

Travis shook his head. "Gordon never said a word."

"Do you want to walk a bit?" she asked.

She took him to the burial plot and knelt to scrape away the ice on the grave stone. Travis knelt beside her in the snow and traced his fingers over the irregular lettering:

MARY COOPER WELLS
WHO KNEW THE SACRIFICE OF LOVE

"I'm so sorry, Lacey," he said.

And she believed he meant it. She swallowed the emotion welling up inside her. "Now I have an idea what it must have been like when you lost your mother."

"And your father?" he asked.

She shook her head. "He's lost without her. He hardly knows what to do with himself. I never knew it would be this way."

"They were together a long time. She was his partner, someone who shared his dream."

Lacey studied his face. The tenderness in his eyes told her that he genuinely shared the grief of the Wells family. But she could not contain her questions any further. "Travis, why are you here?"

"I had to come back."

"Then why did you leave?"

"I had to do that, too."

"You're speaking mysteries, Travis."

"Have you any teaching prospects for next year?" he asked as they began walking back toward the house.

Lacey was annoyed that he had changed the subject. "I haven't let myself think that far ahead. The situation here. . . well, it's too soon. . ."

"So you'll be here?" he said solidly.

She nodded. "I think so."

"Good."

"Why?"

"Because I'll be here. And I'd like it if you were, too."

Lacey's eyes widened. Had Travis really spoken the words

she had longed to hear a year ago? "So how long will you be here this time?" she asked cautiously.

"A long time. I'm going to make Peter help me build a small house and have some of my things shipped up."

"A house?" she echoed.

Suddenly his eyes lit up. "Lacey, that lumber camp is going to be a real town. I've spent the last two months with my father telling him about the peninsula. It's more than we ever hoped for."

"What are you talking about?" she asked.

"My father sent me here on a scouting expedition," he explained. "He's not an ordinary businessman. He has quite a bit of money, actually."

Lacey had already figured that out.

"Father is looking for a long-term investment. I've convinced him of the potential of this place—the lumber, the fishing, the hunting—but we'll need to build roads, of course, to make it more accessible. Someday, soon, I think, we'll build a mill right next to the camp. Only it won't be a camp then, it'll be a town, with houses and shops and families."

"Your father is going to pay for all this?" Lacey said faintly.

Travis nodded. "He expects a good return for his money, of course. I've worked hard to prove to him that building a town is good business venture. But if we put in a branch of our mill and explore the other potential businesses up here, it can be done. We'll create jobs for people who are willing to work hard. Just think, Nathan won't have to grow up alone. There will be friends for Micah, too, and someday, friends for your children."

Lacey blushed. "Let's not get ahead of things. So. . .you're here to oversee this?"

Travis nodded. "I'm here, Lacey. I'm here."

twenty-seven

Surprisingly, the weather cleared. A week after Travis's return, Lacey gave firm instructions that would keep her brothers busy for several hours, and she tromped across the peninsula for a rare winter visit with Abby. There had been no way to send word, of course; she simply could not resist taking advantage of the break in the weather.

Nathan cooed amiably, his colic completely dissipated. He stuck a fist in his mouth and drooled happily. Abby competently balanced him on one hip as she moved about the kitchen, fixing Lacey a cup of hot tea. "Travis didn't tell me you were coming," Abby said, setting the tea in front of Lacey then lowering herself into a chair across the table.

"He didn't know," Lacey answered. "I may look for him before I go home."

"You don't need to look far," Abby said. "He's coming for lunch."

"Here?"

"Yes, he and Peter are going to talk about some plans. Peter is so excited about the idea of building a real town, he can't wait to get started. We were glad to have neighbors when the Stantons moved in, but we need to attract more families to move up here."

"I suppose if you are going to have a town, you have to have people to live in it."

"Maybe someday you'll move over here," Abby mused.

"Oh, I don't know about that."

"But Travis is going to build a big new house. It would be perfect for the two of you."

"I think you're getting the cart before the horse," Lacey said. "Travis and I have no plans to. . .to. . .no plans for anything."

"Don't be coy, Lacey Wells," Abby said. "He's completely smitten with you, and you are with him."

"You're forgetting that two months ago he left without any explanation. He never sent a letter, nothing. Then he showed up again out of the blue."

"But now you understand why," Abby insisted. "He couldn't say anything about developing a town until he knew whether his father was willing to finance it."

"Don't forget that last year he practically forced me to leave, even though he was staying here," Lacey countered.

"You're exaggerating. He offered you the opportunity to do something he thought would make you happy. How can you blame him for that?"

Lacey sighed. "I suppose I can't. But I do wish he would speak more plainly. I really have no idea about his intentions."

"And just what are your intentions?" Abby prodded.

"What do you mean?"

"You have to know your own feelings before you concern yourself with figuring out his." Nathan started to fuss. "I'd better feed my son."

"Can I help you get lunch ready?" Lacey offered, glad for the opportunity to change the subject.

&

An hour later, Peter and Travis burst through the door with rolls of wide paper tucked under their arms. When Lacey heard the door open, she wiped her hands on a dish towel and slowly moved to the front room.

Travis stopped abruptly. "Lacey! Hello! Abby didn't say you would be here."

"Abby didn't know. I've imposed myself upon her without an invitation."

"You're always welcome here, you know that," Peter said. "I'm going to go say hello to my son. You two must have a lot to talk about." Peter left the room.

Lacey turned to Travis and smiled. "I wasn't sure if I would see you today."

"I hope you never come all the way over here and don't see me," he replied. "And I hope you'll come often."

Lacey shrugged. "That depends."

"On what?"

"The weather."

Travis nodded. "That's a sensible approach. "It's only December. We have a lot of winter yet to go."

"Lunch is ready," Abby announced. She laid Nathan on a quilt on the floor, and he promptly began to inspect his toes.

"Abby," Peter said with his mouth full of ham, "you've got to see these plans Travis has been working on."

"I'd love to."

Without waiting to finish the meal, Peter reached behind him and grabbed the long rolls. Travis hastily pushed aside the dishes and unfurled the plans.

"We'll improve the road we already have," he explained, pointing to a line on the drawing. "We'll make it wider. Down at this end, we'll put in a row of shops. We'll need a general mercantile first of all, and then some specialty shops."

"I'm going to open a furniture shop," Peter declared. He grinned. "I won't have to worry about competition way up here, and there's plenty of wood."

"The mill will need offices," Travis continued. "And we'll want a proper medical clinic. I want to have that ready even before we find a doctor."

Lacey's mind harkened back to her conversation with Joshua, when he had announced his intention to study medicine with the hope of returning to the peninsula some day. Had he known that such a grand plan was in Travis's mind?

"My father wants to put up a hotel," Travis said. "But it might be a while before a hotel could be profitable."

Peter disagreed. "People will need temporary quarters while they build houses. We must work on the hotel soon."

Lacey chuckled. "You two almost have me believing this place is a bustling metropolis."

"It will be," Abby interjected. "Just wait and see."

"Just where will all these people come from?" Lacey asked.

"Milwaukee, Chicago, Duluth, lots of places," Travis answered. "We'll start by opening a full-service lumber mill right here, instead of floating the logs somewhere else to be milled. That will mean jobs for men willing to work hard."

Lacey looked at the plans. Travis had drawn in a network of streets fanning out from what would be the center of the new town. He was picturing rows of houses, with a central area for shopping and community life. If his plans materialized, the new town would soon outshine the places like Tyler Creek that dotted the map of the state. Travis's eyes shone with a light she had not seen before his departure.

"This is ambitious," she said aloud.

Travis put his finger on the map. "Over here, there will be a church, a real church. And next to it, a school." He raised his eyes and looked at Lacey. "We'll need a teacher."

"What are these?" Abby pointed to a network of thin lines imposed over the whole town.

"Those are the wires for electric lights."

"Electric lights!" Abby and Lacey said together.

"I know that won't happen right away," Travis conceded, "but some of the big cities are thinking about it. The Pillsbury flour mill in Minneapolis is already using water power to make electricity for the mill. Charles Pillsbury has an electric fan in his office! Why shouldn't the whole city have lights?"

"Next you'll be talking about telephones," Lacey said.

"Exactly! It won't be easy to persuade the telephone company to string wires all the way up here, but we won't give up until we have telephones."

Peter reached for the paper and began to roll it up once again. "I hate to eat and dash off, but I have to get back to work." He glanced at Abby. "Your father wants an exact count of the logs we float today."

"You go ahead," Travis said. "I'll be along in a few minutes."

"I should start back, too," Lacey said. "The boys will be threatening each other with bodily harm if I leave them for much longer, and Papa will not be able to manage."

"I'll walk with you part of the way," Travis offered.

Behind him, where only Lacey could see her face, Abby grinned and nodded enthusiastically. "I would be glad for the company," Lacey said politely.

Outside and down the path a few yards, Travis chuckled. "I saw Abby's face in the looking glass."

"Oh, you mean—"

He nodded. "Clearly she was delighted that I was going to walk with you."

"Abby sometimes gets ahead of herself," Lacey said. "She's always been that way."

"And what is she ahead of this time?"

Lacey's steps slowed. "You. Us. She has us married and living in that fine new house you are planning to build with a half a dozen children."

"Does that seem so unreasonable to you?" Travis asked.

"Well, I. . ." Lacey did not know what to say.

Travis took Lacey's hand and turned her toward him. "Lacey Wells, you have to know how fond of you I am. But I know how much you have wanted to leave the peninsula. And when your brothers are a little older, or your father recovers from his grief, you'll be free to do that."

"I—"

He put a finger on her lips. "Someday there will be a town here, with children who need a teacher. It's really going to happen. But I know it might not happen soon enough for you. If your dream is somewhere else, I don't want to stand in your way. But God has brought me here, and this is where I belong."

She looked into his eyes and knew he spoke the truth. "I'm fond of you, too," she said hoarsely. "I didn't understand why you sent me away last year, until I went. You were right then; I needed to go. But you don't have to send me away again."

He shook his head. "I'm not sending you away. I just don't want to hold you back."

She searched his eyes. Was he saying everything in his heart this time?

He sighed. "Peter will be looking for me. Will you come to the Christmas party?"

"There's going to be a Christmas party?" she asked.

He grinned and nodded. "A real town celebrates Christmas. Come on Christmas day, that is, if. . ."

"If the weather—"

"Yes, if the weather." He released her hand. "I'll see you next week, Lord willing." And he turned and walked back toward the camp.

In a fog, Lacey turned and continued her trek home. When she came to her clearing, her bootprints from a few hours earlier were the only disturbance of the pristine, sparkling covering. The winter sun, low in the northern sky, was nevertheless strong enough to dazzle the air. Evergreens decades old, perhaps even centuries, stood tall and proud, determined to resist the onslaught of winter with full dignity. Suddenly she wondered why she would ever want to leave this place.

twenty-eight

"Is it time yet? Is it time yet?" Micah, already in his coat, pranced around Lacey in the kitchen.

"Just a few more minutes," she said. "Papa's going to make sure the light has plenty of fuel, then we'll go."

"But it's a nice day," Micah protested. "No one will need the light today."

"You can never be sure about the weather, especially in the winter," Joshua replied sternly. He had arrived home only the day before and was already doing his best to help Lacey manage the household. "If we're going to be gone all day, we must leave the light burning."

"We're going to take the cart, aren't we," Jeremiah asked.

Lacey nodded. "The snow is packed down enough that we can pull the cart. If the three of you want to cram into the back, you may."

"Don't smush me!" Micah warned loudly.

"Shhh," Lacey said. "Don't get so excited."

"I don't think we should even be going," Joel said. "We should stay home and have a regular day."

Lacey sighed and glanced at Joshua. Joel had a point. Only a month had passed since their mother's death and it seemed odd to think about observing any of the family's traditions without her. Christmas Eve dinner was a routine chicken with potatoes rather than the roast duck that Mary Wells would have managed. They had not kept the midnight vigil, waiting for Christmas morn with the house lit up with candles. No one had played a single Christmas carol on the piano. Lacey had made all the boys new shirts. Micah was already wearing his, but the twins had opened their boxes only to quiet Micah's incessant nagging and they soon set them aside.

170

For Micah's sake, Lacey had tried to create a festive atmosphere, at least for this one day. Daniel Wells had reluctantly agreed that the whole family could attend the Christmas party at the lumber camp, and the weather had proved no obstacle. He appeared in the dooway and gave Lacey a silent nod. It was time to go.

≈

They arrived at the camp and found it bustling with activity. Abby's mother had conjured up a spread of food reminiscent of Peter and Abby's engagement party. Abby and her neighbor, Lillie Stanton, had surveyed the trees up and down the crude road and designated one as the official Christmas tree. This they had decorated with bows and ribbons miraculously produced from the recesses of their homes.

The boys dispersed and Daniel Wells settled into a chair next to Tom Saget. Lacey had not expected he would want to be sociable; she was not sure she did herself. But it was a Christmas party and she could not very well ignore everyone there. Travis had specifically invited her and he must be around somewhere.

Lacey first went in search of Abby. Scanning the street, she decided that Abby was not likely to have Nathan outside because, although the day was bright for early winter, a brisk breeze chilled the air. Lacey had a fleeting thought that she ought to keep a better eye on Micah. His curiosity might take him too close to some dangerous equipment. She saw his blue coat streak across the dirt road and satisfied herself that he was staying out of trouble.

Abby's house was set back from the main road, and beside it was the small house for the Stantons. At the sight of them, a picture of Travis's meticulously drawn plans flashed through Lacey's mind. Travis was going to build his house a hundred yards beyond the three existing ones, as a token of his hope that the vicinity would one day be filled with homes and families. Lacey could almost imagine what a row of houses would look like, with children bursting out of the front doors on a fine spring day and mothers hanging their wash in the backyards.

She reached Abby's door and knocked firmly. The door flew open almost immediately, and Abby stood before her with bright, excited eyes. "Lacey, I just heard the news! I'm so excited."

Lacey raised an eyebrow. "What news?"

Abby turned away abruptly and began walking toward her kitchen. Lacey followed her in. Nathan smiled up at her from a quilt on the floor. "I told my mother I would bring these sandwiches down," Abby said, "but I haven't quite got Nathan ready. Would you mind taking them for me?" She handed Lacey a platter.

"What were you talking about a minute ago?" Lacey asked.

"Oh, never mind that," Abby said, turning Lacey around at the shoulders, "just take the sandwiches. Mother's waiting. I'll catch up with you later."

Before she knew it, Lacey found herself standing outside of Abby's house with a platter of sandwiches, the door closed firmly behind her. Puzzled, she trudged down the road toward the common hall to carry out her task. Packed snow crunched under her feet and the view was so bright she had to squint. Lumberjacks milled around the road, a couple of them raised their eyes to inspect the platter.

"Mrs. Saget knows how to put out a spread," one said. He winked at Lacey. "I expect we'll have another party before long."

Lacey hardly knew this man. What kind of crude suggestion was he making?

Peter passed by on the other side of the road. He waved energetically and called out, "I'm really happy for you," and kept on going.

Lacey turned and stared after him. *What is he talking about? What is everyone talking about? My mother died a month ago and my father is trapped in a depression. What is there to be happy about?*

Lacey reached the hall. Abby's mother was bustling around

organizing the layout of the food, and she nearly snatched the platter from Lacey's hands as she asked, "Where's Abby?"

"She's coming in a few minutes. Nathan was't quite ready."

"I'm glad you two had a chance to talk," the older woman said. "I'm sure you've got a lot to tell her these days. She's so pleased, utterly pleased." She turned and was gone, leaving Lacey with a question half-formed on her lips.

Retracing her steps, Lacey saw that many of the men were drifting toward the common hall, no doubt expecting that soon they would be free to fill their gullets with the foods that Abby's mother had spent days preparing. Lacey began to look around for her brothers. With her eyes raised to peer down the street, Lacey did not notice Micah hurtle toward her. He jumped into her arms, nearly knocking her off balance.

"Micah!" she said, startled. "What's gotten into you?"

"Why didn't you tell me?" he demanded.

"Tell you what?"

"You know, what everyone's been saying. Why didn't you tell me first?"

Lacey set Micah down on his feet. "What are you talking about, Micah Wells?"

"You're going to marry Travis!"

Her mouth dropped open. "Where'd you hear such a thing?"

"It's all over the camp. Everyone's talking about it."

Suddenly all the odd looks made sense. "Well, everyone is quite mistaken," Lacey said, lowering her voice and shepherding Micah away from the growing crowd outside the common hall.

"Don't you want to marry Travis?" Micah demanded.

Lacey sighed. "It's more complicated than that. Besides, he hasn't asked me."

A throat-clearing noise behind her made Lacey spin around, and she stared into the eyes of Travis Gates.

"But I meant to," Travis said softly. "That is, I still mean to."

Lacey's mouth dropped open again. "Mean to what?"

"Ask you to marry me, of course."

Lacey glanced around. People were staring at them. "Apparently you are quite confident that I will say yes."

Travis shrugged sheepishly. "I'm sorry about all the fuss. I told only Peter."

Lacey laughed. "And he told Abby, and she told her parents, and her father told a few of the other lumberjacks."

Micah tugged on her arm. "It's true, isn't it?"

"Please make it true," Travis said. "Marry me and build a life with me. . .build a town with me."

"Do it, Lacey!" Micah urged.

Lacey swallowed hard and looked into Travis's eyes. "I think I'll do just that."

A Letter To Our Readers

Dear Reader:

In order that we might better contribute to your reading enjoyment, we would appreciate your taking a few minutes to respond to the following questions. When completed, please return to the following:

Rebecca Germany, Managing Editor
Heartsong Presents
PO Box 719
Uhrichsville, Ohio 44683

1. Did you enjoy reading *Tend the Light?*
   ❏ Very much. I would like to see more books
      by this author!
   ❏ Moderately
      I would have enjoyed it more if _____

   _____

2. Are you a member of **Heartsong Presents**? ❏Yes ❏No
   If no, where did you purchase this book? _____

   _____

3. What influenced your decision to purchase this
   book? (Check those that apply.)

   ❏ Cover   ❏ Back cover copy

   ❏ Title   ❏ Friends

   ❏ Publicity   ❏ Other_____

4. How would you rate, on a scale from 1 (poor) to 5
   (superior), the cover design? _____

5. On a scale from 1 (poor) to 10 (superior), please rate the following elements.

    ___Heroine   ___Plot

    ___Hero   ___Inspirational theme

    ___Setting   ___Secondary characters

6. What settings would you like to see covered in **Heartsong Presents** books?_____

_____

_____

7. What are some inspirational themes you would like to see treated in future books?_____

_____

_____

8. Would you be interested in reading other **Heartsong Presents** titles?   ❏ Yes   ❏ No

9. Please check your age range:
    ❏ Under 18   ❏ 18-24   ❏ 25-34
    ❏ 35-45   ❏ 46-55   ❏ Over 55

10. How many hours per week do you read? _____

Name _____

Occupation _____

Address _____

City_____ State _____ Zip _____